"What in the devil is happening?"

Beatrice looked toward the open study door and felt...everything shatter. It was not merely her brother and a few colleagues; it was a house tour. Complete with some of the sharper-tongued gossips of the *ton*.

And then she looked up, up at the man who held her in his arms, to see familiar blue eyes. Far too familiar.

The stars. The sun.

Briggs.

His hand was still planted firmly on her buttocks, and suddenly the warmth of his body became an inferno, the strength of his hold a revelation.

She could not breathe.

You can breathe. No man is allowed to steal your breath.

Even so, the fact remained...

She had flung herself at Briggs. And her brother had walked in just in time to see it.

Author Note

Beatrice and Briggs's story has been in my head in some form or another for quite a long time. I loved the idea of a woman setting out to ruin herself—only to be ruined by the wrong man...who turns out to be the right one. But further to that, the idea of a sheltered young lady and a rather dominant duke fitting together just perfectly is something that's been sitting there in my imagination for a while, waiting for the right moment. Bea and Briggs were definitely the right moment.

I have always loved dukes. I don't know what it is about them. Perhaps it's the same reason I love a billionaire hero in a contemporary. I love a man with seemingly endless power brought down by the love of a woman who might—for all the world—seem so much less powerful. Yet, in the end, his heart beats for her. And that makes her the most powerful of all. Because love is the most powerful of all. More powerful than dukes, or society, or scandal.

I hope you enjoy this story as much as I enjoyed writing it.

MILLIE ADAMS

———

Marriage Deal with the Devilish Duke

HARLEQUIN®
HISTORICAL™

Recycling programs
for this product may
not exist in your area.

ISBN-13: 978-1-335-40733-7

Marriage Deal with the Devilish Duke

Harlequin Enterprises ULC
22 Adelaide St. West, 40th Floor
Toronto, Ontario M5H 4E3, Canada
www.Harlequin.com

Printed in U.S.A.

Millie Adams has always loved books. She considers herself a mix of Anne Shirley (loquacious but charming and willing to break a slate over a boy's head if need be) and Charlotte Doyle (a lady at heart, but with the spirit to become a mutineer should the occasion arise). Millie lives in a small house on the edge of the woods, which she finds allows her to escape in the way she loves best—in the pages of a book. She loves intense alpha heroes and the women who dare to go toe-to-toe with them (or break a slate over their heads).

Books by Millie Adams

Harlequin Historical

Claimed for the Highlander's Revenge
Marriage Deal with the Devilish Duke

Millie Adams also writes for Harlequin Presents.

Visit the Author Profile page
at Harlequin.com.

Chapter One

1818

There were not many things a woman could control in the world. Her life determined not so much by the winds of fate as the whims of men.

But there was a point where Lady Beatrice Ashforth decided that while she could not be the ultimate queen of her own existence, she could be the architect of her own ruin.

And in the end it would amount to very much the same thing.

Her brother, Hugh Ashforth, the Duke of Kendal, might have control over many things, but only so long as she behaved.

She was through with behaving. The life that Hugh wanted her to live stretched out as grey and unending as a mist on the fields of the Bybee House grounds, the house she would never leave if her brother had his say.

She would never have a Season. She would never...

Marriage, he had decreed, was not something she need concern herself with.

For she was taken care of.

Her brother had consulted a physician—the one who had cared for her in her childhood—on her continued good health, and it had been the opinion of the doctor that childbearing would be the death of her.

That had been all her brother had needed to hear to decree that she should stay beneath his protection.

Beatrice was concerned with her freedom.

She had spent her childhood shut up in the walls of Bybee House. Everything from fresh air to rain to too much sunlight was deemed the enemy of her health.

When her father had died, the responsibility for her health had fallen to Hugh. Hugh did nothing by half measures.

He cared a great deal for her happiness. He brought her sweets from London whenever she wished, new dresses, beautiful bobbles for her hair.

That was precisely why she'd come up with her scheme. One she had told no one—not even Eleanor, her brother's ward—about.

Well, she had told one person. Her accomplice in the plan.

But she trusted James. His family had purchased a country manor within proximity to Bybee House four years earlier and the two of them had fallen into a strange sort of friendship.

She had never expected to befriend a man. She knew it was somewhat unseemly for a young lady. But Beatrice was accomplished at sneaking out. It had been the only way she could ever have fun as a child. The only way she could leave her bedchamber.

More than that, she had sensed that…it was where she might find her strength. Lying in bed, endlessly bled by physicians, confined to rooms with low light. She felt as if she were withering away. A flower starved for the earth, the rain and the sun.

Out there she had found strength she hadn't known she'd possessed. It was how she had met Penny, who had once been destined to be her sister-in-law, until the engagement to Beatrice's brother had been broken. And ultimately, she had found James, and a deep friendship with him.

That friendship had led to conversations about marriage. He was having issues around the subject as well. He did not want a wife, in truth, and though he had not been able to explain it all to her—he had stumbled over his words and in the end asked if she could simply believe him—they had discussed a potential solution for them both.

She would have freedom. She would have a life, a real life. A life as a woman, rather than simply as her brother's shut-in sister for the rest of her life.

At least tonight the party was at the house, which meant she would be permitted to be in attendance. Though, she was not treated as a real guest. She did not dance. Or have a dance card. Had not made her debut in society.

For after all, what was the purpose?

Hugh did not wish her to marry. And so, he did not have any plans to bring her out. It all made her feel so desperately sad. So desperately lonely. As a married woman she would be permitted to attend balls. She knew she was playing a very dangerous game. That her reputation would be poised on the edge of a knife, and the wrong interpretation of the moment, the wrong strain of gossip, the wrong timing, could damage her in a way that made things quite difficult. But she was invisible as it was, and she would rather be ruined than non-existent.

'You look beautiful,' Eleanor said.

Her friend was lounging on the settee in the corner, dressed in a delicate silver gown covered in glittering stars. Eleanor was to debut this Season. She would not be formally presented in court, as her father had not been part of the aristocracy. Bea didn't know the full circumstances surrounding Hugh's connection with Eleanor's family, only that he had been named her guardian and she was now his responsibility.

Well, Beatrice was his responsibility as well, and he had made decisions about her life that were far too high-handed for her to endure.

'Thank you,' Beatrice said, looking at herself in the mirror.

She liked the dress that she was wearing, but she did not look beautiful in the way that Eleanor did. For Eleanor was allowed to look like a woman.

And Beatrice still… She was not in a sophisticated ball gown, not in the way that Eleanor was. Her hair was not pinned up in the same fashion. But it did not matter. For Beatrice was going to make her own way. Her brother was a duke, and he was powerful. And he prized propriety above all else.

He had been engaged a year prior to the daughter of an earl. And when he had heard rumours of her affair with a Scottish soldier he had broken the engagement off swiftly. Coldly. Her brother was a good man, and she knew it. His care of Eleanor was evidence of that. But he had absolutely no tolerance for impropriety. Not after the way their father had treated their mother. He had made a mockery of honour, and Hugh despised it.

Which made the game she was about to play tonight all the more dangerous. Hugh would see her married to James after this. But he would be… He would be deeply disappointed in her. He would not understand. As far as he was concerned he was the head of the household, the head of the family, and what he deemed to be right and true and necessary was so. Her brother was arrogant, all the way down to the soles of his boots.

He was a duke. No one dared question him. No one except for his best friend, the Duke of Brigham, whom they all called Briggs.

They were as different as two men could possibly be. They might have the same title, but their behaviour, their outlook on life, was quite different.

He would understand. When she explained to him. If she was allowed to explain it to him. Ever. If her brother didn't actually kill her.

Though, she doubted he would, considering he was pushing her to this place out of his concern for her untimely death.

'You seem distracted,' Eleanor said.

'I am rather,' Beatrice said. 'I only hope that tonight is…' She could not find a word for it. 'Fun.'

What a silly, nonsensical word for planning to upend your whole life.

Eleanor smiled, but the smile seemed sad. 'I am sure that it will be. Your brother is intent on finding a husband for me.'

'You don't sound happy about it.'

She smiled and it did not reach her eyes. 'What I want is impossible, Beatrice.'

Beatrice's heart crunched slightly. On behalf of her friend. If there was one thing that she knew about Eleanor it was that... Well, she knew that Eleanor was in love with her brother. It had been clear when Hugh had become engaged to Penny last year.

Oh, Eleanor had been lovely to Penny. And she had said nothing. But the devastation was evident behind her eyes.

Beatrice had never felt it was at all appropriate to mention it. For no matter how true her feelings were, no matter how real, they were doomed. Hugh would no more return her affections than... Well he would not. For many reasons. Propriety, the title... He would have in mind a very particular sort of woman to be his Duchess. She knew that about her brother. He had very particular ideas. And they would not include Eleanor or her feelings.

But then, her brother's plans never did. They did not take into account the feelings of others, only what he assumed to be right. When his former fiancée, Penny, had explained to Beatrice the truth of the situation— that she had not had an affair with a Scottish soldier, but that her father had sold her to him to pay off his debts— Beatrice had believed her. Whether or not her brother had... It hadn't mattered. The damage had been done. And there was nothing that could have been done about her marriage. In the end, Penny had agreed to marry the Scot and go with him back to the Highlands. But the truth didn't matter. Not to Hugh, whose opinion of Penny had been altered forever.

Once Hugh determined someone had fallen short, they could never again be held in the same esteem they had been before.

That could be her after tonight.

Yes. It could be.

But she had two options. She could either go along with what her brother wanted for the rest of her life, or she could attempt to claim something for herself.

And so she had decided on this endeavour, dangerous though it was.

She knew that the reputation of a woman was a perilous thing. And that becoming ruined was actually much easier than remaining beyond reproach.

'Shall we go downstairs?'

'Yes,' Beatrice said. 'Let's.'

It was just time for guests to begin arriving. Beatrice wanted to make sure that she was tucked away in an advantageous corner of the ballroom so that she could watch for the arrival of James. And from there, she would decide the best course of action. Because she would have to figure out exactly where she had to be seen with James. And what exactly they needed to be doing.

She was not entirely certain how tonight would unfold, and she needed to…think. Needed to get a sense for what was happening.

She took a sharp breath and steeled herself, as she and Eleanor walked down the stairs. Their feet didn't make a sound on the rich, burgundy carpet that covered the stairway. Marble from Italy gleamed bright on the floor of the entry, reflecting the lights of the elegant chandelier that hung above. Intricate scrollwork carved into the crown mouldings.

But it paled in comparison to the opulent ballroom. The marble there was gilded at the seams, frescoes

painted on the walls and the ceilings of angels and demons locked in heavenly battle.

They moved from the entry into the ballroom, and
Beatrice immediately set upon the punchbowl. She was
quite pleased to see that there were already refreshments
placed out, and that there were a few people in attendance. Her brother would arrive on time. Not a moment
sooner or later. What was fashionable did not matter to
him. It was a matter of being a man of his word.

When the ball truly did start, Beatrice was relegated
to the back by her own sense of propriety. She was
a guest without truly being a guest. In many ways it
was actually shocking that Hugh allowed her to come
downstairs and attend in any measure at all. He could
have just as easily kept her shut up in her room. But
he did not.

It was quite the break with tradition. By Hugh's stan-
dards.

James was not here yet, but she knew that he would
be. And soon. Her brother arrived, made greetings to
his guests. And eventually made his way to the back
of the room.

'How are you finding this evening?' Hugh asked.

'Lovely. As ever,' she said, fighting the urge to twist
her hands with nervousness. He would ask what was
wrong if she displayed a hint of nerves. He was far too
perceptive. It was not part of his charm.

His eyes darted behind her. 'Where's Eleanor?'

'I do believe that she was asked to dance,' Beatrice
said.

'Was she indeed?'

'Yes.'

Her brother's gaze was sharp.

And she could see that his concerns would be transferred elsewhere. She did wonder sometimes, if he believed so strongly in the force of his own will that he did not worry about her defying him, or if he simply did not believe her to be a woman. If he did not believe that anyone would ever see her that way. It was entirely possible that he believed he did not have to guard her against suitors because he did not believe that she was capable of having any.

He saw her as a *sickly child*.

The thought made her very sad. Deeply so. And sometimes when that despair welled up inside her she…

Her chest felt heavy. And she ached. That clawing feeling that she couldn't breathe overtook her and she worked hard at her trick. One she had cultivated on those long days spent ill. Was it her body denying her breath through restricted airways or fear making her think it was? If she slowed the moment, the world, she could find the truth. And so she did, relaxing her shoulders and breathing in deep. Then she dug her fingernails into her palm, the slight pain soothing.

Pain was an interesting thing.

At least, in Beatrice's opinion. Some avoided it, and she supposed that was its purpose. To tell you to turn away from a path, to warn you of harm.

But she hadn't had that choice. Pain was part of saving her life, part of the regimen doctors used on her body.

She'd had to forge a different way of relating to it.

It marked so many steps taken in her life. Good and bad. She had been bled as a child. Frequently. It had been excruciatingly painful. Many of the treatments she'd been subjected to had been. And then, as her health had begun to improve, she had taken what opportunity she could to sneak out and roam the estate. That was how she had met Penny. She had found her lost on the estate, having wandered too far from home.

Beatrice had been loath to let anyone know that she had been out, as she hated to reveal her secrets. But she had found a great deal of freedom and pain out in the world, when she had finally been able to explore nature. Bee stings and the sharp pain of falling and scraping your knee. Falling out of a tree.

All things that she never wanted her brother to know had occurred. But she had begun to associate it with her liberation.

And sometimes... There was a familiarity to it that hurt. It was not something she spoke of. Not ever. For it made little sense, even to herself. Yet as her nerves began to fray she found balance in the pain in her palm. A sort of grounding sensation.

A sense of strength.

A sense that she knew herself and that she could withstand far more than anyone believed. It was that sense that gave her confidence now.

She felt a strange prickle at the back of her neck, and she looked up, just in time to see Briggs walk in.

The Duke of Brigham.

When he walked in, a ripple went through the room. Briggs was the sort of man who attracted attention wherever he went. It was undeniable.

He was magnetic in a black coat, black waistcoat and white cravat. He wore buckskin breeches and black Hessians. In a room full of men dressed in similar fashion he should not be notable. But whether it was the fit of the clothing, or simply the quality of the man beneath, he was more than notable.

He was outstanding.

He was the most beautiful man Beatrice had ever seen. She was certain he was the most beautiful man anyone in this room had ever seen. And the reaction to him indicated that. But it was not just his appearance— though his dark hair, kept just long enough to carry a slight wave, and his piercing blue eyes were certainly the pinnacle of masculine attractiveness.

No. It was his bearing.

He carried an air of authority that was unquestionable. He was an entirely different man to her brother. Not one bound quite so tightly by honour. And yet. And yet there was never any doubt that he was in absolute control. Of himself.

The *ton* had an obsession with him, as did every marriage-minded mother. If he had a fault, it was that he was already in possession of an heir. But his marriage had been brief, and many years ago, so much so his bachelorhood was firmly re-established.

As was his reputation as a rake.

But he was also…kind. And she had always found him easy. Easy to talk to. Easy to befriend. She knew he did not think of her as a friend. She would be little more than a child to him, for as long as he'd known her. But she carried a deep well of affection inside herself for Briggs, and whether or not it was sensible or reasonable, it remained.

It was…

She felt sometimes as if the stars hung on his every word. And that the sun shone because of his every breath. She would not say that she carried a flame for him, not in the way that Eleanor did for Hugh. No. It wasn't that. Briggs was beyond her. It was simply that she… That she could not imagine her life without him. And in that way, yet again he was like the sun or the stars. Unreachable, but it was unfathomable to imagine life without that warmth. That presence.

He did not acknowledge her. Not formally. In fact, he crossed the room and made his way to a group of ladies. Not debutantes.

Widows.

Men of his sort preferred widows. They did not have to observe the same strictures as young ladies. Beatrice could not pretend that she understood the nuance of that. She felt a strange prickling sensation though, watching him as he spoke to those women. And then he turned, only slightly, and his eyes met hers from across the room.

And he winked.

Her heart jumped in her breast, and she turned away. She did not want him to look at her for too long. She had the fear that he might be able to suss out that she was up to something, and the last thing she needed was to be caught out by Briggs.

She nearly fainted from relief when she saw James arrive. He was wearing a smart grey coat with a blue waistcoat, the effect overall much softer compared to Briggs's much more severe attire.

He was sweet and handsome, angelically so. With blonde hair that curled at the base of his neck, and pale blue eyes.

She did not feel… What she did not feel was as if a magnet drew her to him. As if she could not look away from him. She felt comforted by him.

Friendship.

Theirs was a deep and real friendship. One that—were it known about by the *ton*—would see her ruined anyway as she had been alone with him without a chaperon before. Now they would simply need to court public ruin.

In the absence of her brother's blessing, she would have to force his hand. Because he hated scandal above all else. Which meant… She would have to create one.

And he would never see it coming, because he did not believe her capable.

James came to her, a second glass of punch in his hand.

'Are you thirsty?' He handed it to her.

She appreciated it. The care it demonstrated. He was like that. He was kind.

'Thank you,' she said.

'Have you devised a scheme for the evening?'

'I have to figure out where I think we might be seen and by whom. Logic indicates that it should be Hugh who catches us out.'

'I see. And are we to simply wait in his bedchamber?'

For some reason those words made her stomach tighten. 'His bedchamber? I do not think we need a bedchamber.'

The look on James's face was almost…pitying. 'Perhaps you're right.'

'A lady can be ruined by walking along the wrong garden path,' Beatrice pointed out. 'I could have been ruined long ago if it was known I went calling at your residence and took tea in your drawing room without the presence of a chaperon.'

'I rather think that for the scheme you're devising

there was going to have to be a measure more than *walking* involved. Or taking tea. There can be no doubt as to what is being witnessed.' He looked down. 'I fear your brother enough to know he must think the only option is for us to marry, lest I find myself called to account, and on the wrong end of his pistol.'

She looked up at him, feeling helpless. Because she did not know *what* he was alluding to.

She was… She was terribly sheltered. And she had seen pictures in some of the books left in the library that depicted nude nymphs running away from male suitors, and it always made her feel uncomfortable. For some reason, those images came back to her now, and she had a feeling… Well, she had always had a feeling that something to do with those images related to *ruin*. It was only she could not connect them.

'I should like… I…'

He smiled, and it was kind. 'I do not wish to force you into anything, Beatrice. Please, if you wish to turn back, it will never be too late.'

'This is for you as well,' she said. 'You also must feel…you also must have the life you desire, James. And I care for you. If I could help you, I wish to.'

And she might never be able to understand exactly why he didn't want a real marriage. And perhaps the two of them would be giving up certain things. But they would have friendship. And all the freedom marriage afforded.

And she… She had felt for him. Because while he was a man, he was a second son, and he did not have anywhere near the power that her brother had in his position in society. He was facing enormous pressure from his family, and it was a pressure he did not want.

Beatrice didn't have to have experienced the exact same thing to understand what it was to be presented with a life you did not want to live.

'I know,' she said. 'I know what to do. It would be best to have the largest audience as possible, while seeming to believably seek isolation. I know where to go. We will be found, not only by my brother, but by his associates.' Briggs would be among them. The very idea made her skin feel scorched. Shame. She felt a deep sense of shame.

'He often retires to his library at some point during an evening such as this,' she continued. 'If we could contrive to be in present...and...'

'We should only have to be locked in an embrace,' James said. 'That should be enough.'

She felt somewhat mollified by that. A simple embrace did not seem so ruinous. But she knew that to the broader society it would be seen as such.

'Yes,' she said. 'I believe that is so.'

'We shall meet there.'

'Yes. And in the meantime, endeavour not to draw suspicion.'

She waited. Waited until the hour drew closer for her brother to begin to make his way from the ballroom. They would have to get there before him. With a bit of time.

James was already gone.

She swept from the room, taking care not to be seen, and tiptoed up the stairs, towards her brother's library.

The only light in the room was that cast by the fire in the hearth. She hoped that the staff would not precede her brother to light candles for those who would soon occupy the room. The staff might offer her discretion. She did not want discretion.

She wanted to be ruined.

She sensed movement in the corner, and she turned, her stomach tight with nerves, her entire body nearly surging with unnatural amounts of energy. And then she heard footsteps. Just at the same time. And before she could think, before she could do anything but act, she did so. She flung herself at the figure in the corner, wrapping her arms around him. But he was so much taller than she had expected him to feel.

So much more solid.

The figure…the man…moved against her, and she nearly fell backwards. And then he lowered his hand, cupping the rounded globe of her buttocks. And she knew that hand was *much too large* to be James's.

Terror streaked through her, but just then, the door flung open wide, and along with the open door, came the light.

'What in the devil is happening?'

She looked towards the open study door and felt… everything shatter. It was not merely her brother and a few colleagues; it was a house tour. Complete with some of the sharper-tongued gossips of the *ton*.

And then she looked up, up at the man who held her in his arms, to see familiar blue eyes. Far too familiar.

The stars. The sun.

Briggs.

His hand was still planted firmly on her buttocks, and suddenly the warmth of his body became an inferno, the strength of his hold a revelation.

She could not breathe.

You can breathe. No man is allowed to steal your breath.

Even so, the fact remained...

She had flung herself at Briggs. And her brother had walked in just in time to see it.

'I demand an explanation now. Or I will have no choice but to call you out.' She could see murder in her brother's eyes, and she knew that he was not speaking in jest.

'There is nothing untoward here.' Briggs released his hold on her slowly, ensuring that she did not fall.

'And yet, we have all witnessed something quite untoward, sir.'

'It's my fault. It's my...'

'There is no question. There is no question of what must be done.'

She looked back at Briggs, who was gazing at her brother with fury in his eyes. 'Of course.'

'What's it to be. Pistols at dawn?'

'No,' Briggs said, his voice firm. Decisive. 'It is to be marriage.'

Chapter Two

Philip Byron, the Duke of Brigham, was not a man to be trifled with. He was not a man easily bested, nor was he a man to back down from a challenge. But at the moment he felt thoroughly bested, by a chit barely out of the nursery. And were there reasonable challenge to be had in the current situation, he would gladly undertake it. But the only man in the world that he considered a true friend was currently glaring at him with clear murder in his eyes, and Briggs was well aware that when it came to the honour of his sister, Kendal would follow through with that murder.

Kendal was hardly a prude. The man took his pleasure when he wished. Briggs knew that better than most. They frequented clubs, gaming halls and brothels often enough. But that was just it. When it came to pleasures of the flesh, Kendal kept it separate from his family. And he certainly did not go about despoiling ladies. Neither did Briggs, for that matter. And he would never, ever have touched his friend's sister. It was she who had flung herself at him. But at the current moment, there was no space to say so.

He regarded Kendal closely. 'Might we see that your sister is safely ensconced in her chamber and continue this conversation in private?'

'No,' Beatrice said, scrambling even further away from him. 'I don't need to be ensconced. I wish to speak to you, Hugh, we must…'

'Do not speak to me,' Kendal said. 'Neither shall you speak to me,' he said to Briggs. 'Not until I have had a chance to…'

'I'm sorry,' Kendal said to the group of waiting guests. 'I must adjourn the tour. I bid you please make use of my hospitality further. But I would also ask that you refrain from speaking on the matter that you think you have witnessed here until we are able to set it to rights.'

The entire group dissipated at Kendal's command, for he was, after all, the Duke. But Briggs knew that there would be gossip. That it was unavoidable. The damage was done. And it did not matter what had truly happened.

'Hugh…'

'Go,' Kendal said. 'Go to your bedchamber, and we will speak later.'

'I wish to speak now.'

'I will not hear you now.'

'But please I…'

Kendal held up his hand, and he could see that Beatrice was weighing her options. She could persist. She could say what she had to say between his denials. Or she could wait until he was in a better frame of mind. And when she demurred to Kendal's commands, Briggs did think it was likely the better of her options.

She left the room, and Kendal closed the door behind him.

'Explain this to me.'

'I was simply standing there. I do not know who your sister thought I was, but I swear to you, that I have never, and I would never...'

'Good,' Kendal said. 'I know exactly what manner of man you are in your relationships. I should not like my sister exposed to any such thing.'

'Have no worries, Your Grace. I have not exposed your sister to my appetites.'

The air seemed less deadly in the aftermath of that admission.

'You have an heir already,' Kendal said, looking at him closely.

Briggs felt a stab of discomfort over the mention of his son. It was true. He had already achieved the highest purpose of his life. He had sired an heir. The line would continue. It did not matter that he had been ill-suited to marriage, always and ever. That he had no idea what to do with the child, particularly not one with the difficulties his own had. But he was receiving good care and a fine education.

What else could be asked of him?

'You must marry my sister,' Kendal said.

'You believe that I did not touch her.' That was important. Briggs had very few people in his life he considered friends.

He had not been allowed at school until he was fourteen. So ashamed had his father been of his behaviour and so intent had he been on crushing Briggs, to remake him into something he could control, something he could understand.

When he finally had been allowed at school it had been after his father had died.

His mother had sent him.

'You're the Duke now,' she'd said, her voice still soft from years of tiptoeing around his father. *'You are no longer simply Philip.'*

And he had not been Philip. Not once since.

He'd become the Duke of Brigham, wholly and completely. He had made a new man of himself. Briggs.

Ironically, that was what his father had wanted all along and it had taken the bastard dying for Briggs to accomplish it.

Still, he had not found school easy and the process hadn't occurred overnight. When it came to friends...

In truth, he had precisely one.

And it was Hugh.

Hugh sighed and turned away from him, as if gathering his thoughts. Or just perhaps reining in his desire to punch Briggs in the face.

He imagined, had he been anyone else, Hugh would have attacked him on sight. It was only the strength of the connection between them that he didn't. Hugh had been Briggs's first friend, and in the end, he felt that Hugh was the only true friend he had even now.

While he might understand the rules to society now, while he did not require Hugh to act as a guide any longer, he did not feel a connection to anyone else.

In truth, he knew Hugh felt the same. They'd both had the full weight of their titles thrust upon them far younger than they should have. They had navigated those dark waters where boys became men. And the rarer passages of boys becoming dukes. And they had done so together.

It was that history now which kept Briggs from certain death and he knew it.

Also what kept him back from challenging Hugh in return, a defence of his own honour justifiable under the circumstances.

It was not his fault Beatrice had thrown her body against his.

A body that was quite a bit softer than he had ever allowed himself to imagine…

'Yes. Because I do believe that you are man of honour, and you would at least confess your sins, even if you had sinned in such a manner.'

'If you will not believe that I would never compromise your sister, then please do believe that virgins have no interest for me. If you will recall, I have already had a lady wife who could not bear me.' He did not speak of Serena. Ever. It was a mark of just how exceptional the situation was that he did so now.

'What happened with Serena was not…'

'I do not need your reassurance, Kendal, particularly not when I stand before you with the choice of marrying your sister or taking your bullet. It is rather duplicitous, do you not think?'

'You're my friend, even if I would like to shoot you at the moment.

'Honour is everything,' Kendal said.

'I know. And you know I share your feeling. I understand why you must see the world as you do, given the way your father set about salting the earth of morality while he drew breath. But you must not think it would be a good thing for your sister to…'

'A marriage in name only,' Kendal said. 'Society will

never have to know of your arrangement. You have always been good to her. Protect her, as I wished to do.'

'Do you not think your sister might have something to say about that? You consigning her to a marriage only in name?'

The alternative…well, Briggs could not see it. His father had died when Briggs was so young, he had been resolute in his need to marry and produce an heir as quickly as possible. He had married Serena when he was twenty-one. And had lost her at twenty-three.

He had been infatuated with Serena and he had been so certain…

He had been so certain love would grow between them. If not love, at least a friendship.

He had been naive.

He had interpreted her mercurial nature as something exciting. The scope and change of her moods like a tide. So stark was the ebb and flow of them that he could read them easily.

But they became erratic. The high of them often as unsettling as the low, which could last months. And eventually became all that remained.

It was only after his marriage with Serena had deteriorated to the point she no longer spoke to him that he realised he'd been…a romantic. He'd believed that she would be the one person he could be himself with.

He had met Beatrice when she was a girl, and had felt instantly drawn to the child who was nearly a prisoner in her bedchamber. He so rarely felt compelled to reach out to people around him. And truly, he did not often need to. He was a duke. People were desperate to reach out to him, and it made his life all the easier for it.

But she…

He had wanted to make her smile. In a world that seemed very determined to give her nothing to smile about.

If there was one thing he had understood, it was what it was like to be born into a life you had not chosen, and that felt ill-suited to your nature. And so he had always paid her visits when he'd come to call. Had always brought her sweets from London.

He had recognised a rebellion in her eyes, and he had felt a kinship to her. For he had been much the same. In the wrong life, the wrong family. Perhaps the wrong bloodline. Never meant to be the heir.

She had been placed in the wrong body. One that could not contain the wildness in her spirit. One he wholeheartedly supported.

Until, of course, it ensnared him.

Still, he would never have sentenced the poor creature to a marriage with him.

One of the many, many ways in which he was wrong included what he desired from women. He had been young and foolish and he had believed that his wife would…that as she was a virgin when she came to his bed he might—in time—introduce her to his preferences and she would share them.

Nothing could have been further from their reality.

In the years since his wife's death, many women had enjoyed their time in his bed. But those women were not *ladies*.

Ladies, marriage…

All of that was supposed to be behind him.

'You can continue to do whatever you like,' Kendal continued, as if a wife was an incidental hardly worth overthinking. 'You already have your heir. And Beatrice will have…a child to care for should she wish it. She… She desperately wants that. I know when the doctor told her that it was not advisable that she bear children she was deeply upset.'

'She cannot have children?' Briggs had not been aware of that.

'She *should* not. That is my concern. She very *likely* can. But you know how her health was in her childhood, and it is the opinion of those in the medical profession that she would take a great risk to bear children. It was why she was not to make her debut this Season.'

'That's what you told her?' Briggs asked.

'Yes.'

'What *exactly* did you tell her, Kendal?'

'That she would not need to marry. That she would not marry. Because I would take care of her. And of course I will. She is my responsibility. It is my responsibility to keep her safe.'

He could see his friend had no real idea of what he'd done, and further that he…did not know his own sister.

Beatrice was sweet, it was true. But she was also quietly determined. And she was not half as biddable as she appeared. Over the years he'd stayed at Bybee House on many occasions and he knew Beatrice was often *not* where Kendal assumed her to be. He had seen her appear at dinner out of breath, with red cheeks from being in the cold, and occasionally a leaf somewhere in her tangle of brown hair.

But of course, his friend's largest shortcoming centred around the idea everyone took his authority as seriously as he did.

His little ward, Eleanor, she hung on his every word.

His own sister on the other hand…

'I see,' Briggs said. 'So, what you've done is create this situation we find ourselves in, while laying blame everywhere else.'

'*How* have I created the situation?' Kendal asked, clearly outraged.

'You offered your sister a life sentence. Living here at Bybee House in the country, away from society, from friends, from freedom. I don't know why she chose to target me as her means of escape, but she has found it, hasn't she?'

'What exactly are you saying, Briggs?'

'You sent the lady from the room, so we cannot *ask* her. But do you not suppose that she was taking matters into her own hands? Now she is ruined. If I don't marry her my honour will be worth nothing. If you don't call me out as a result of this ruination, your honour will be nothing. If Beatrice does not marry, she will be... Well, she will never be received in society, will she? Not that you were to allow her out. She is, of the three of us, the one who stood to lose the least.'

'You do not think...'

'I am telling you that I have never laid a hand on your sister. And somehow, she came to be in my embrace in this study, which, I believe she knows you make use of in the evenings following such gatherings.'

Briggs could see the wheels turning behind Kendal's eyes.

'Shocking though I know you find it,' Briggs said. 'Not everyone agrees that you know best. Clearly, Beatrice is among that number.'

'*Beatrice,*' Kendal said.

And this time it was her name that held the tinge of murder. Kendal turned and tore from the room, and

Briggs went after him, because after all, why should he not? He had already ruined the lady, why not accompany her brother to her bedchamber?

They wound down the labyrinthine halls of the massive estate, Kendal's footsteps announcing his outrage against the marble floor. He flung her doors open, and a maid, who had been kneeling by the fireplace, immediately scurried away.

Beatrice was laying on a chaise, looking collapsed, which gave Briggs a strange sort of squeeze in his chest. He had come to know Beatrice when she was aged fourteen or so, and had not known her in the worst part of her illness. And he had to wonder if this was how she had looked then. Pale, drawn, and not infused with the sort of life he had come to associate with her.

She sat up, her face swollen, her eyes red. She looked distraught, so much so that it would nearly be comical were it not for…everything.

'Briggs,' she said. 'Please know that I did not mean…'

'You did not *mean* to entrap Briggs?' Kendal asked. 'Then who, my sister, did you intend to be caught with tonight?'

'Hugh…'

'Do not think me a fool, Bea, I know that this was a plot of yours.'

Of course, Briggs had been the one to tell him that. But it was not the time to comment on such a thing, he was certain.

Kendal continued, 'Who did you intend to be trapped in a marriage with, Beatrice?'

'Had I been caught with James rather than Briggs you would never have known it was a plot…'

He curled his lip. '*James.* James. That friend of yours from the country estate next door?'

Beatrice tilted her chin up, intending to look imperious, clearly. It was not terribly effective, given the tip of her nose was red. 'Yes.'

'His father is a *merchant*,' Kendal said.

'His father is an *earl*. The same as Penny's, and you were going to marry her.'

At the mention of his former intended, Kendal's face went to stone. 'That is of no import. That is enough for me. It is not enough for you.'

Beatrice swung her legs over the edge of the chaise, the motion sudden and not at all ladylike. 'You were not even going to allow me to marry, so what concern is it of yours the title of the man that I choose?'

'I feel we are perhaps having the wrong fight,' Briggs said. 'As he was not going to allow you to marry, and now you cannot marry this…this *boy* anyway.'

'I'm sorry,' she said, turning her focus back to him. 'I did not know that you would be there. I expected for James to be there already. But he was not and… It was you.'

'This is dangerous,' Kendal said. 'And foolish. You were playing with things that you knew nothing about. What you have done… You have potentially damaged yourself beyond saving. You *have* to marry Briggs, but that does not mean that society is going to be kind to you. You were caught in his embrace. Unfortunately for you, the wrong sort of people, the worst sort of gossips, saw. And from where I was standing the embrace had the mark of the obscene.'

Briggs snorted. Because, honestly, it was becoming theatrical. 'I dare say that it looked nothing like obscene to *you*, Kendal. You might be playing the prig in front of your sister, but you and I both know that you have seen and participated in more decadent pursuits of a common afternoon, let alone a night in an empty drawing room.'

And yet, the impression of her luscious roundness remained in his hands, and he had to confess if only to himself that it felt a bit like *obscene* where the sensation lingered.

'Not,' Kendal bit out, 'with a lady.'

'Beatrice is more than suitable to be my Duchess,' Briggs said. 'And I will not tolerate a bad word spoken about her, in society or this room.'

He did not know why he defended her. Not in light of everything.

Perhaps it was *because* of what she had done.

It was foolish. Ridiculous. And exceedingly brave. She had risked much to defy her brother.

Had she done it for love? The love of this... James?

He looked at her, at the misery on her face.

He did not think she had. She was not *heartbroken* now, but furious.

She had done it to kick against Kendal, and for that he could only feel a grudging sort of respect.

From infancy, there had been a clear path laid out for Briggs. All he had to do was marry and produce an heir, and the rest... It was his choice.

Beatrice was beneath Kendal's authority. And she had limited options when it came to opposing it. None of what her brother had was hers. Nothing would ever pass into her ownership. She would have to acquire a husband to ever change her circumstances, and Kendal had taken steps to ensure she could not do so.

So she had defied him in the only way she could. Forced his hand.

In truth, he was angrier at his friend than he was at her. In this, he understood her. The desire to have one's own life. To make one's own choices. All while being thoroughly misunderstood by those around you.

In his case, actively despised.

'A duchess?' she said. 'I don't want to be a duchess. I just want to marry James. I want to be free. And I want to have a life of my own. I didn't want to stay here for-ever. I already made an entire life of these walls. And I could not take any more of it. You took everything from me, Hugh, when you said that you would not allow me to marry. When you withheld presenting me to court, having my Season. I… I did not have a choice. I told you then that I could not bear it and you did not listen. And now you cannot simply hand me off to Briggs…'

'What I *offer* you is an honour,' Briggs said, the re-ality of the situation not quite yet settling in. For it was too much to fathom. Beatrice. Beatrice as his wife. Him taking a wife a second time…

He had never intended such a thing.

Perhaps William needs a mother.

William had a governess. William…

Was the angriest, most difficult child he had ever known. He had terrors in the night, and destroyed all of his toys. He did not speak fluently, and he was vol-atile at the best of times. It was only because he had managed to secure a very esteemed governess that any-thing went as well as it was currently. She was a sturdy woman with a capable manner, and years of experience. She had informed him that she had known children like William before. It was her opinion that he would grow well enough, though would potentially always have a different sort of manner about him.

The boy had support. He did not need a mother.

William had had a mother, who had not cared enough about him to stay.

Just as Briggs had had a father who had hated him.

At least he loved his son.

You leave him to his governess more often than not...

But he did not scorn him.

Surely that had to count for something.

'I am preserving your reputation the best I possibly can,' Briggs said. 'And my own. You have given me no choice in the matter, Beatrice.'

'I will secure a special licence,' Kendal said.

Briggs snorted. 'I am more than capable of securing my own special licence, Kendal. Or do you forget that you do not outrank me?'

He caught his friend's gaze, and held it for a moment.

He did wonder sometimes, if Hugh forgot. That they were not now schoolboys. That Briggs no longer required his protection, his guidance.

'I have *not* agreed to marry you,' Beatrice said.

Briggs looked down at her, and saw that her eyes were filled with tears. Perhaps he had misread her.

'Did you fancy yourself in love with James?' Briggs asked. She said nothing, though her misery seemed to increase. He felt almost sorry for her. 'You will recover.'

'Get some sleep,' Kendal said. 'There will be a wedding to plan on the morrow. And we will have to inform Mother.'

Chapter Three

Beatrice was desolate. Everything was wrong. And worst of all, she didn't even know who to speak to about it. Or if she could speak to anyone about it. That was how she found herself slumped in the morning room with nothing but cold meats and eggs for comfort.

It was then that her mother came in.

'Beatrice,' she said softly.

It was the softness that nearly broke her.

But everyone was soft with her. Always. Except for Hugh last night. And Briggs had not looked particularly soft either.

Her heart gave a great thud.

Briggs. She was to marry Briggs. In three days' time. And suddenly, she felt overwhelmed by all she did not know.

About him. About the world. About what was to be between a husband and a wife.

'You're crying,' her mother said.

Beatrice touched her face. There were indeed tears on her cheeks. She had not realised.

'Did he hurt you?' her mother said, drawing close

to her. She reached out and put her hand on Beatrice's. 'Has he…forced you into anything? I will not consign you to an unhappy union, Beatrice. I know that your brother thinks that it's best but if he…'

Beatrice shook her head. 'He did not hurt me.' Hurt? Being held by Briggs had been the furthest thing from hurt. She had avoided thinking of that moment, but now it loomed large in her mind. 'I am the one that ruined everything. I am the one that caused this.'

Her mother looked at her closely. 'How exactly did you cause it?'

She explained her plan to her mother. Her ultimate rebellion against Hugh. 'And I could not tell anyone because you would stop me. But I… I am not as weak as everyone thinks I am. I have… I have dreams. There is a purpose to why I survived my childhood. I nearly died so many times, but I did not. And if I'm simply to live out all my days here at Bybee House, I don't know…'

'Oh, Beatrice.' Her mother put her hand over hers. 'Hugh does not mean to hurt you in any way. It's just that he worries for you.'

Her mother loved her, and she knew that. She also knew her mother had spent years deep in the throes of a relationship with Beatrice's father that had been anything but easy.

In those years, her mother had often been withdrawn. When her father had flaunted his many infidelities, her mother disappeared into her chamber and did not emerge. Or worse, into laudanum.

She had overheard her mother say to a visiting friend once that being married to the Duke would not have been so awful if she did not loathe him and desire him in equal measure.

Beatrice had not understood what it meant. She still did not.

But in the years since her father's death, her mother had emerged much stronger. Much happier, and Beatrice had never wanted to do anything to disturb that.

'I know it. But this was more than protection. And I had to do something about it.'

'It is a good match,' her mother said. 'He is a duke. He is well liked in society…'

'Yes.'

She didn't know why, but he also frightened her. On some deep level. As much as he drew her to him. And she had not intended to embroil him in this.

'He deserves better. Than me.'

He had lost a wife already. Beatrice did not know what ailment had taken his first Duchess, but to be married to a woman who had been told she might not… Be strong. She had not intended to steal any chances from him and a happy life. She and James had an agreement. An understanding. Briggs had not been part of it, and he did not deserve this.

'His honour will not allow him to let this all fall upon you, dear.'

'But it *should*,' Beatrice said. Then angrily disagreed with herself. '*No*. It should fall on Hugh. Because he is the one who forced me into this position. He is the one who made this untenable. And I… I'm just so sorry. I care quite a lot too much about Briggs for this to… For this to be his fate.'

'Beatrice, we must speak. And you are getting married in three days and…'

'Yes?'

'There are things that a married woman must do. There is… A duty in being a man's wife.'

Beatrice tried to imagine what duties that might entail when one was married to a duke who surely had a full household staff. Well, her mother saw to a great many domestic activities.

'I must help run the household,' Beatrice said.

'Beatrice,' her mother said. 'I mean there is more than that. It is only that you will be expected to…'

'Yes?'

'There is the marriage bed.' For a moment her mother's face took on a distant quality, the expression in her eyes something fond and sad and angry all at once.

And just when it became too sharp to bear, it eased.

'What happens between a husband and wife in the bedchamber,' her mother continued.

Bedchambers. James had said they ought to be caught in a bedchamber. And then she thought of nymphs again.

And of her governesses. All young and pretty and fluttery and more interested in her father than in her.

'Oh.'

'It is not so unpleasant. Your husband will…know what to do and he will take the lead.'

'Like dancing?' she asked.

Though she had been given lessons in dance.

Her mother looked relieved. 'Yes. Like dancing. He will lead you, and he will ensure that all is well. As you said, he is a good man.'

'What… What am I to *do*?'

She wished she knew…anything. She felt like a great blank space was stretched before her and all she had

were scattered images and ideas, and what she wanted
to do was demand answers.

What made a true marriage?

What happened in bedchambers?

Why were women so easily ruined?

Why had she felt like she had when he'd held her?

She had the sense these things connected, but she
did not know how. And it was an endless frustration at
what was denied her.

She had been so protected here at Bybee House. She
was never permitted to go to London. Her father had
died when she was a girl and her brother remained unmarried. She had seen interactions between unrelated
men and women only at the handful of balls her brother
had given and even then it was like…

Watching a pantomime.

It gave only hints and ideas and just enough to be
maddening.

'You can think of other things,' her mother said.
'Pleasant things.'

Think of *other* things. That was what she did when
she was forced to engage in needlework. She thought
of anything but the project she was currently involved
in, as it was untenably boring.

It simply did not sound like anything she might want
a part in. And was another resounding point in favour of
the facade marriage she had been planning with James.

James.

She would have to speak to James. He undoubtedly
had heard.

The door to the morning room opened, and their butler appeared. 'His Grace the Duke of Brigham is here
to call upon the Lady Beatrice.'

Beatrice's heart gave a start.

'I suppose I should stay and offer to be your chaperon. But I feel it is a trifle too late. I will let you speak with him.'

Beatrice wanted to call her mother back. Tell her no. Because she was terrified of being alone with Briggs at this current moment. Which was silly, because she had never been terrified before. But she doubted that today he would be bringing her sweets. She doubted it very much.

He had been in her bedchamber last night, and apparently there was something scandalous in that. Last night she had been too upset to truly consider that.

He swept into the room, somehow she could tell he was wearing a different coat than the night before, though this too was black. He looked like a storm. And everything in her went still. She couldn't breathe.

Her mother dipped her head. 'Your Grace.'

'Your Grace,' he returned.

And then she left them in there. Alone. And the doors closed firmly behind her.

'Briggs…'

'We must speak. About the reality of the situation that we find ourselves in.'

'Of course,' she said. 'I know that we do. I know that…'

'You need not fear anything from me. I am aware of your condition.'

'My condition?'

'Your brother has informed me that you were not to bear children.'

'I…'

'I have an heir. Already. That will not be an issue.'

That made her desperately sad, and she didn't even know why. Presumably, she and James would not have had children. After all, theirs was to be a presumptive marriage in name only. Not a true marriage, he had said. She did not know exactly what that meant, but she did imagine that it precluded offspring.

'You look distressed.'

'James…'.

'Yes. Are you going to try to tell me that you loved him?'

'And if I did?'

'I would not believe you. For you threw yourself into my arms easily enough. You let me hold you. You did not seem to realise I wasn't your beloved.' He fixed her with his dark gaze. 'You would know the arms of the man that you loved, Beatrice.'

And she remembered the way he had held her again. The way his hand had slid down over her rear, and she felt horrible, scalding heat go through her body.

Another clue, she felt.

But he was not asking for a true marriage. He had an heir.

It is not different than James, then.

And yet it felt as if it was.

'James is my friend,' she said. 'And the idea of marrying for convenient reasons suited him.'

'Marriage is only ever convenience, if it is not, it is an inconvenience.'

'Some people fall in love,' she said.

Except she had never known anyone who had. She was quite certain that Eleanor loved Hugh, but there was no reciprocation. And there would be no marriage.

'That is very rare, Beatrice, and even if they do…
It does not last.'

She wondered, then, if he was speaking of his wife.
Of course, it hadn't lasted. She'd died. Beatrice had
never known her. She had not seen Briggs at all during
his brief marriage. They had been mainly in London.
She had never met his son either.

A strange, twisting sensation assaulted her stomach. His son.

Would she be his mother?

Everything was changing so quickly. She had an idea
in her mind of what it would be like to marry James. He
had said that he wished to travel abroad, and she was
quite amenable to that. She had looked forward to seeing Paris, and Italy. To spending time in London. All
things that she had never done. She had been cosseted.
She had been kept to herself. With him, she knew that
she would go to more social engagements. And together
they would enjoy themselves. For she did enjoy his company very much. She liked Briggs. She always had. But
it was different. It was simply different.

Everything about him was different.

One of the many things she had no name for.

'Your brother wishes us to marry here. In the church.'

She nodded. 'Yes. That… That would be fine.' She
had not thought about where her wedding would take
place. Not even when she had concocted all of this with
James. She had not given further consideration to any of
this. Not really. She had pictures in her mind of a life.
But she had not truly thought about what all this might
entail. Yes, she had thought that she had been prepared
to face Hugh's ire, and that was something. But there

were so many other things along the way that she had not fully considered.

She curled her fingers into fists, stabbing at her palms, as she bit the inside of her cheek, looking for that sort of grounding that occurred when she was able to overcome pain.

But then, there was a strong grip on her chin and she found her face being tilted upwards. She met his eyes. Those dark, shockingly blue eyes, and she felt…

Calm. Quiet.

As if the storm inside her had been halted by the touch of his hand.

'You have nothing to fear from me.'

'I know,' she said.

Her breath was at a standstill, her heart suspended in her chest. And then he moved away, and the world began to move again.

'You look frightened.'

'I'm not,' she said.

A lie.

His gaze was cool, and filled with reproach. Unfamiliar. For she had seen Briggs largely in good humour throughout her acquaintance with him. But then, when would she have had occasion to see him otherwise? But she had not seen him look like this. She had known it was there, though. She had sensed it. For had she not seen the way that he drew people to him? That he commanded all the attention in the room.

Authority. He wore it like other men wore overcoats.

'You are lying to me,' he said.

And she wondered if he had been able to read her mind.

'Sorry,' she said, lowering her head. 'I did not mean to lie.'

She looked up at him from beneath her lashes, and she saw something flash in his eyes. Something she had no name for, but that created a strange sensation low in her stomach. 'You must tell me,' he said. 'You must tell me the truth, Beatrice. It is important.'

'I promise. I am frightened. Because I don't know...' She searched for the right word. But there really was only one. 'Anything.'

He chuckled. 'You need not concern yourself with anything.'

'Why aren't you angry with me?'

Of all the things, that made the least sense. Why he was not filled with rage. For she had forced his hand into something that he gave no indication he wanted.

'Because it makes no difference to me, Beatrice. I have the resources to care for you.'

'But if you wished to marry...'

'I did not,' he said, clipped. 'As it has been previously stated, I have my heir. There is no reason for me to ever marry again, and I had no intention of doing so. However, you shall be as my ward.'

'Your... Your ward?'

'Yes. As I said, your brother has explained everything to me.'

'I'm not free.'

This was the second time in the space of very few hours that he'd looked at her as though she was an object of pity. 'Darling girl, there was never a question of you being free. You would belong either to your brother or to your husband. That is the way of things.'

And then he turned and left her standing there, feeling as if he had poured cold water over her head. Because he was right. She had been seeking freedom... But she could not own anything. She could not make her own way. She had been seeking freedom by means of tying herself to another and…

And that meant there would never truly be freedom.

That was how she found herself running blindly through the estate, making her way to James.

When she arrived at the house, her hands were muddy, and she was in a state. But she did not care. His housekeeper admitted her quickly and ushered her into the sitting room to await him. She had been Beatrice's accomplice from the beginning. Supporting and encouraging their friendship, though she was not sure why.

It was only moments later that James came into the room.

'Are you hurt?' he asked.

'No,' she said. 'I'm engaged. Which at the moment feels tantamount to the same thing.'

'Dammit, Beatrice…'

'I'm sorry,' she said. 'I've made a mess of this for everyone.'

'Don't be foolish, you daft girl. I don't care about myself. I care about you. I'm not being forced into marriage. And I never was. It was an opportunity to help you and to deal with my father, but it was never a necessity. Not in the way it was for you.'

'I feel so terrible…'

'Beatrice,' he said. 'Sit down with me.'

'I will.' She sat. But then she immediately wanted to stand back up. So she did. 'I cannot,' she said. 'I have too much energy.'

'All right. Then we will both stand. Beatrice, my problem is not that… I can trust you. Yes?'

'Of course you can. I was going to marry you.'

'Yes,' he said. 'I know. And I should have told you this before you were committed to that. But I did not want you to change your mind. I did not wish to lose your friendship.'

'You cannot lose my friendship.'

'I might yet. But I will… Beatrice, I do not wish to have a true marriage with any woman. Because I do not have… I do not have the ability to love a woman.'

'Why do you think that?'

'Because I wish… When I think of my life. When I imagine who I might find happiness with… It could only ever be a man, Beatrice.'

She felt… She did not know what to think of that. She did not know what to make of it at all.

'Oh. But you cannot do that,' she said.

'No. It is against the laws of the King. And I could be imprisoned for it. Or killed.'

'Oh.' Yet again she felt as if there was something she was missing. What did anyone care who James wished to give his heart to? Why should there be laws? It made absolutely no sense. 'I do not see why it should matter. Should we not all be able to find our own happiness? Why can we not? Briggs told me today that I would never find freedom. And he was not being cruel. He was correct. I cannot find freedom because as a woman I can never own anything. All money that is given to me is charity. The houses I live in belong only to men. And when I marry Briggs… He said I will be his ward. Not his wife. And that is his determination to make be-cause… He is a man. But you're a man also,' she said. 'You cannot be free either, can you?'

'Beatrice…'

'Why is it that only certain people are allowed to have happiness?'

'Beatrice, I cannot begin to understand why the world works in this way. What I do know is, as long as people like you, and people like me, are determined to be happy, we will find ways. We do not need the permission of others. I'm thankful that you are my friend. That you look at me, and you feel no judgement. But you were willing to be my wife as you were.'

'I wish I still could be,' she said.

'You care for Briggs,' James said. 'I think perhaps more than you know.'

'What do you mean?'

'You watch him. Whenever he's in any room, and it cannot be held against you, mind, as he is a handsome bastard.' James smiled, and his cheeks turned slightly pink. 'But it's more than that. You like him a great deal.'

'Of course I do. He's always been kind to me.'

'I think you are drawn to him.'

'I don't understand.'

His smile was full of sympathy and she hated it. She was extremely tired of being surrounded by men who understood more of her own future than she did. 'You will. When you go to live with him. I think it is possible that with Briggs you will find more than you could have with me.'

'I cannot. For he's set on honouring my brother's wishes.'

'That is if he does not find it difficult.'

'I am very tired of not understanding what it is people are saying. Or not saying. Or trying to say.'

'I'm sorry,' he said. 'Please stay my friend. I think

I'm going to go away to London. Without you here...
There is little reason to stay.'

'James...'

'I love you, Beatrice.' He smiled again. 'Not as a
husband.'

'I love you a great deal as well,' she said. She nearly
said not as a wife, but then, she still did not know exactly what that meant. And yet somehow... She knew
she didn't.

'I will be there for you. As a friend.'

'Thank you,' she said.

And whatever else might happen, she knew that she
had him. And that mattered. But she was left to turn
over what he had said about Briggs. About her feelings for him.

And there was no satisfactory answer anywhere inside her.

Chapter Four

It was the eve before his wedding and Briggs found that he could not sleep. Not that a wedding was overly consequential to him.

Particularly not one to Beatrice.

Beatrice...

She was sweet. But what an insipid word it was for her.

An image of her face, her expression fiery, filled his mind. And it was more than just the image of her. It was the feel of her.

When she had thrown herself into his arms as a woman flinging herself off a cliffside. Heedless, determined.

Fearless.

Soft...round in all the places a woman should be.

He tightened his jaw, his hand clenched into a fist.

She was not sweet. Look what she had done in the name of gaining her freedom.

Poor girl.

She had got herself tied to him, and while he saw no purpose in altering the course of his life over her misstep...

Her life would change.

Or perhaps it wouldn't. Perhaps it would be much the same. But her dreams might be just slightly crushed.

For she had sought a life she would not find with him.

He stood from the chair he was seated in and walked over to the window, looking out over the estate. It was dark, the tops of the trees rustling. And in the shadows, he could see a flash of movement.

Something white fluttering in the wind.

He watched the strange, haunting movement for a moment.

Then, found himself walking out of the bedchamber, and down the stairs. He did his best to minimise the echo of his footsteps on the hard floor. He walked out through the front door, and turned to the right, following the walls of the great estate home, out towards where he had been facing. It was a clear night, and the air had a bite to it. And he did not know why he was compelled to chase ghosts outside his bedchamber window.

Perhaps he preferred them to the company of the ghosts that he found inside it.

He stopped there, at the edge of a grove of trees, and he could still see the fluttering white. Moving forward and backwards. Closer and further away. He took a step forward, then another. And suddenly realised.

'You could catch your death out here,' he said.

'Briggs?'

He had been right. It was Beatrice. He could not mistake her bright, starlit voice. It was like silver.

As he got closer, he understood what he'd seen from

the window. She was suspended on a swing that hung in the centre of the grove of trees.

'Lucky for you. Not a highwayman. Or anything else intent on stealing whatever fortune you have on your person or your virtue.'

Her virtue.

He should not think of her virtue.

And yet, it was difficult to avoid thinking of it altogether. Her brother had concerns about her bearing a child, but there were many ways to find pleasure...

It was far too easy in that moment to imagine her as the virgin sacrifice in her white nightgown. Far too easy to imagine her sinking to her knees before him...

You will not be teaching her the ways you find pleasure.

She would be disgusted. Likely go screaming right back to her brother, who would ensure Briggs lived out the rest of his days as a eunuch.

'What are you doing out here?'

'I thought I saw an apparition outside my window.'

'I am not an apparition,' she said. 'I am just Beatrice.'

'A relief.'

Her hair was loose; he had never seen it so. Falling over her shoulders in thick, heavy curls. She was pale and wide-eyed in the moonlight. Like a virgin sacrifice to be taken by the gods.

But not by him.

'I am... I am considering my life in your servitude, Your Grace.'

'Servitude?'

'I'm not free. Was that not the discussion we had mere days ago?'

'You will be freer with me than you ever have been

before,' he said, and at the same time he wondered if that were strictly true. 'You will have the protection of being a married lady. Scandal will not be able to touch you quite so easily.'

Though because of her health… She would not have all the freedoms that she might've had otherwise. But he would not say something. Not now. Not when he was trying to comfort her. A task he was unequal to. For he was not one to offer comfort to anyone.

'And what sort of freedoms will I have?'

'What do you wish, Beatrice?'

She closed her eyes. 'I wish to see things. More than this place. I did not ask for this,' she said. 'I did not ask to be ill. To be fragile. It is an insult, I feel, that my spirit does not match my body. For I have always felt that I…' She closed her eyes and tilted her head back, a shaft of moonlight illuminating her skin. And he could see that her nightgown was…

Transparent.

Even in the dimness of the moonlight he could see the shadow of her nipples, the faint impression of dark curls between her thighs.

She was like a goddess. Beautiful. Untouchable.

Absolutely untouchable, no matter that he was to be her husband.

He had married a woman so like her. Serena had been fragile. Beautiful. Virginal. And utterly unprepared for him. Their life together had not been happy. In fact, he felt, unavoidably, that he was part of her being driven to such despair that she could no longer live.

The one person on earth he had attempted to connect with. The one person he had attempted to find a real relationship with and it had…

He had not loved her. But he had thought that he might one day. He had been ready to fight for that. To make it his aim.

But in the end, he had disgusted her. He had told her he would change. That he did not need to indulge himself.

She'd said now that she knew, she could not see him the same again.

She'd barely tolerated intimacy as it was.

'When I read stories, I imagine myself as the heroine. I can see myself slaying dragons and defeating armies, riding a horse through the fields as fast as possible, and... Falling in love. But then to be told that my body cannot do those things... How is that fair? Why could I have not been given a sweet, retiring nature? There are many women who are happy to be home. Who are happy...' She shook her head. 'Of course, I don't suppose any woman wishes to be told she cannot have children.'

'Some might see it as a path of ultimate freedom, in many ways,' he said.

'What do you mean?'

The sadness of Beatrice, the thwarting of her plans, the realisation that he was...

That he was the master in her life now, that all compelled him to offer her something. To speak, even when it hit against sharp places in his soul.

'When you have a child, your cares will be with them always. Your life will never fully be your own. To have another person placed in your care like that is to never truly have your heart beat for itself ever again.' He swallowed. 'At least that is my experience of it.' He did not speak much of fatherhood. But for him it was...

A painful reminder of his childhood, and he could not escape the feeling of shortcoming that he had now either. He did not know sometimes how to reach his son.

'It must be wonderful to love like that,' she said.

'I don't know that *wonderful* is the word I would use.'

'Well, I will never have the chance, will I? Except... I will care for your child, Briggs. I will. I promise. I will be his mother, if... I'm sorry, I do not wish to bring up memories of your late wife. And I do not wish to cause any hurt. But...'

'I do not hold in my heart a deep grief for Serena. Do not concern yourself with my feelings.'

'I just should not wish to erase her memory.'

'If William cannot remember her then it is her own fault.'

He could see that she was confused by that, but she did not ask, and he did not offer explanation. Of course, the fact that the late Duchess had taken her own life was something that was rumoured among the *ton*, and it did not surprise him that it had not trickled down to Beatrice.

She had cut her wrists in the bath. Her maid had found her, the screams alerting the entire house to the tragedy.

He remembered lifting her from the water still... being covered in water and in her blood.

And the sorrow.

The sorrow of having failed someone so very deeply.

Serena, but also William.

Her family had gone to great lengths to pay to have her buried in the church graveyard. He could admit he would not have done so. His grief had been nearly as intense as his anger, and his concern had not been in where she might be laid to rest, but on what he might tell his son.

Her family had worried only about the disgrace.

They had paid handsomely for her death to be called a drowning. An accident.

Though there were enough rumours in the *ton* about the truth of it. They only wished to whisper behind their hands and fans, about the Duchess burning in hell.

They did not behave in a way so bold as to speak of it openly.

It was the cowardice in that which bothered him most of all. That those people had no such principles as to allow themselves to expose their meanness so boldly and loudly.

It was, he thought, the greatest tragedy of their society.

The way certain things were hidden. It did not make them less prolific for all their concealing of such vices. All manner of bad behaviour flourished in the world. It was only those who should be protected from it who were left ignorant of its existence, and therefore susceptible to brutality.

'Then I shall do my best for him,' Beatrice said, determined.

'He is a… He is a wilful boy,' Briggs said. 'He is not terribly affectionate. You may find him difficult.'

He felt disloyal saying such a thing, but it was true. If she was expecting an easy path to dealing with the void she felt over not being able to have children of her own, she was likely not going to find it filled in his house.

'I do not have a perfect idea in my head of what it means to have a child,' she said. 'I was warned against fantasising about such things, and so I didn't. I will not find it difficult to love who he is. There is no idea of him built up in my head as to what I feel he *should* be.'

Her words, just then, were a revelation. For wasn't that the true enemy of happiness? Expectation that could not be met.

He was well familiar with it. Far too familiar.

He moved closer to her, and then behind, grabbing hold of the swing and pulling it back. His knuckles brushed her hair, soft and silken. And he could smell her skin. Rose water and something delicately feminine that he could not place.

Perhaps it was simply Beatrice.

He released the swing, and she floated gently forward, her hair streaming behind her. And when she came back, he caught her, holding her steady, lowering his head and whispering in her ear, 'I think we will find a way, don't you?'

He released his hold on her again. He could not decide if prior to this he would never have put himself in this position with his friend's sister, never would've been alone with her, or if it would not have felt…weighted.

Because he had been somewhat isolated with Beatrice on any number of occasions. Here at the house, they had not been so formal. Kendal had trusted him, and he had never once moved to violate that trust. And would not have. But he was marrying her now, and whether or not it was to be a real marriage, it had shifted the positioning of their relationship. Had shifted the way he saw her.

Forced him to realise that she was a woman.

On that thought, she returned to him.

'Will we?' She turned to face him, and it brought her mouth perilously close to his. It was plump, and soft looking. In that moment, he felt an undeniable sense of the tragic. For it was possible that for her protection, no man would ever taste that mouth.

No man would ever be able to tap into that passion that existed beneath the surface of her skin, for it did. And that he had always known. It was perhaps why he had always favoured her. Why he had brought her sweets from London.

Why he had taken the extra time to talk to her. Because she was trapped here at the estate, and there was so much more to her than she would ever be able to express. She was right. Right then he could feel it. The storm beneath her skin that she was not allowed to let out. She was staring at him, her eyes filled with questions that were not his place to answer.

He could feel her fury. Her fury in the inability to get those answers.

Poor Beatrice.

'I do not intend to make you miserable,' he said.

'But you will not take me to storm armies either, will you?'

'The primary problem with that,' he said, releasing hold of her again and letting her fly through the air, before bringing her back to him, 'is that I do not know at present where there are any enemy armies, on my life.'

'Surely you can find some, Briggs. I have great confidence in your abilities.'

'In my ability to start a war?'

'Yes.'

'Should you like to be my Helen of Troy, Beatrice?' he whispered, far too close to her ear, as he brought her back to his chest, her scent toying with him now. 'Shall I launch a thousand ships for you?'

He pushed her forward again. 'But I do not wish to sit at home,' she said, looking back as she drew away from him. 'I wish to fight.'

'It is still the same result, is it not? A war, all for a woman.'

'I imagine I nearly started a war between you and my brother.'

He continued to push her on the swing, allowing her to fly free before bringing her back. Only ever letting her so far. So high.

'He believed me easily enough.'

'Because he does not think me capable of anything truly shocking,' she said.

'Because he trusts *me*,' he said, wondering right then if he was worthy of his friend's trust. For as he brought her back, through the swing back, he ended up pressing the warmth of her body against his.

And he could feel the softness of her hair against his chin. And he knew that he was going to have to visit a brothel when they returned to London.

As a newly married man, he would be visiting a brothel.

He nearly curled his lip. Disgusted with himself.

But then, that was the state of things. He was not necessarily proud of the man he had become. But he was not waging a war against his nature either.

And in this instance it was a kindness to his wife.

For many reasons.

'I'm sorry,' Beatrice said. 'Of course that is true. I did not think of it that way.' She let out a slow breath, and he could feel it shift her frame. Then she leaned her head back, and it came to rest upon his chest. She jumped, but did not move. And he simply held her there, his hands gripping the ropes on the swing so tightly he thought he might cut his skin open. 'Am I unbearably selfish?'

His chest felt tight. The rest of him felt…hard.

'You are selfish, perhaps,' he said, his voice rough. 'But we all are. And the world favours the selfishness of men. You did what you thought you had to.'

'I would feel better if you were angry with me,' she said.

He laughed. 'I apologise for not being able to accommodate.'

He released his hold on her and she made a small sound of surprise as she went careening forward. But his heart was thundering too hard, and he should not hold her against his body that way.

'Why can't you be angry with me?'

'Because my freedom is not in question. I will continue to do exactly as I please. As I have always done.'

She laughed softly. 'You've already told me that isn't true. You have a child. Your heart does not beat simply for you.'

He had nothing to say to that, so he pushed her again on the swing.

Beatrice felt breathless. She did not know why. Not breathless in the way that had marked her childhood. Breathless in a way that frightened her.

This breathlessness was not unpleasant. Being close to him was not unpleasant. He had a solid presence that made her feel… Quieted. She had always liked being around him, but this was different. Leaning her head on his chest had felt natural, though she knew it was not proper. She was past proper. She had failed at being proper; she had gone and ruined herself, hadn't she?

He pulled the swing near him again, and she could feel the heat from his body. She felt warm herself.

Her heart thundered almost painfully. He moved his hands, his fingertips brushing against her shoulders, and she shivered. She could sense his strength, and she wanted to lean into it. To test it. In a way that she was never allowed to test her own.

Tears stung her eyes. Because she felt like she was on the verge of something that she would never fully be able to immerse herself in.

Never fully be able to understand.

She turned her head again to look at him, and most of all to chase that strange prickling feeling she had felt before. When she had turned to face him on the swing and their faces had been so close. She was closer to Briggs than she had ever been to a man before. Well, with the exception of that moment in the library when he had put his hand on her hindquarters.

'I would give anything to taste that sort of freedom,' she whispered. 'To know what it's like.'

'People do things… To find that,' he said, his voice low, shivering over her skin in a way that left her feeling shaken. 'To find that sense of pushing against the edges. They take themselves to extremes. But it is not always advisable.'

'Who gets to decide?' she whispered.

'I suppose whoever has the greatest interest in keeping you safe.'

'I sometimes wonder, though, at what point you must abandon safety in order to live. I feel like men are so rarely asked to make these choices. Or at least, if they must, they are the ones in charge of those decisions.'

'Sometimes you have to trust that those who care for you might choose a better path for you than you would choose for yourself.'

He meant him. He meant choosing for her. 'Why must I trust that?'

'I do not have a good answer for you, Beatrice.'

'That is disappointing. You have no anger for me, and you have no answers for me.'

'No,' he said. 'I do not.'

'We are to be married tomorrow.'

'Yes,' he said.

'I do not know what it means to be a wife.'

'You do not have to know what it means to be a wife,' he said. 'You will be a wife to me, and there will be a specific way that can play out. But I will make sure you know everything to do.'

And amid all the uncertainty she found that promise supremely comforting. It was all she had to cling to. And cling to it, she would.

Chapter Five

Briggs had managed to procure the licence easily
enough. And he had gone back to Bybee House, though
his housekeeper had asked him if he wished William
to come to the wedding.

'I should not like to disrupt his schedule.'

'You do not think he might wish to see you married?'

The only reason that Mrs Brown could get away with
speaking to him in such a way was that she had been
with the house since he was a boy. And she had certainly spent more time with him than his own parents.

'I do not think that,' he said. 'He would find it dull,
and the trip would only be taxing.'

And so he was now at the church, prepared to do
what he must.

There would be few people in attendance. Beatrice's
mother, he assumed Kendal's ward, as she was good
friends with Beatrice. And Kendal himself, of course.
But other than the minister, he did not imagine there
would be another.

No one was in attendance. Not yet. He walked out
of the sanctuary, and through to the back, where there

was a small garden, and a stone bench. And upon it sat his bride.

He had last seen her on that swing, with the night drawing a protective veil around them.

It was bright and clear out this morning.

He could see her perfectly well, too well. And the vision mingled with the intimacy of the night before. The way she smelled. The warmth of her body pressed to his.

She was dressed in blush, the gown cut low, as was the fashion. But he had never seen Beatrice in *such* a fashion. She was…

She was a stunning picture there, her elegant neck curved, wisps of dark curls falling down over her pale skin. And her breasts…

She looked up, eyes wide. 'Briggs.'

'What are you doing here?'

'Oh, I escaped. I thought I might come early and…'

'Thank you for telling me the truth.'

He had not been imagining it. The same thing he had seen in her eyes in the library… He could see it again now. She liked to please him. She liked being told what was expected of her.

And that should not intrigue him.

He knew better than to visit his inclinations on a lady. These were things he had attempted in his first marriage, and he had since learned the marriage bed was not the place for such activities. There were brothels that catered to men of his tastes specifically. And everyone involved knew exactly what to expect. And even, enjoyed it. That was the thing about his particular desires. They might be hard, uncompromising.

He might enjoy being in charge, and doling out punishment where it was due. But a woman's submission was only enjoyable if it was given willingly.

And if she received pleasure from the act.

Beatrice would never understand.

He would be very surprised if she understood much of anything about the dynamic between men and women. Ladies were so sheltered. He had experience of such a thing with his first wife. But Beatrice... It was likely she was even more so. Off the country as she was, and with a family that had no intention of ever marrying her off.

'You told me that you wanted the truth. And so I am committed to offering it to you.'

'Good.'

She blushed. And he would be lying to himself if he did not admit that it was an incredibly pretty blush.

'Where will we go?' she asked.

'To Maynard Park. My family home.'

'Oh.'

'We will go to London for the Season. I must see to my duties at the House of Lords.'

For him, the Season typically marked a month-long period of work and excess. As he was not participating in the marriage market, he did not play games unless he was required to attend balls out of deference to a political pursuit. He took his duties relatively seriously. After all, a man had to possess some purpose in his life, or what was the point of it? It was far too easy to be a man in his position and do nothing, care for nothing. To simply exist, as he had much power and wealth, and it was easy for him to do so.

But that was not the way that he saw the world. He would not say that he was an extraordinarily good man, but he did not see the purpose in occupying his space if he did not try to do something to improve the state of others.

'Oh,' she said, immediately looking pleased. 'I do so wish to spend the Season in London. I have not been.... But one time. And never for an entire Season.'

'I have a home there that I feel you will find comfortable.'

'That's wonderful.' She smiled slightly. 'I am... Is it wrong that I'm pleased?'

'It is a life sentence, Beatrice. You can either look at it as if you're going to the gallows or... Enjoy your time in the dungeon, I suppose.'

Badly chosen words on his part.

'I must do my best to enjoy it.'

But she looked a bit pale and uncertain.

He felt rather than heard the approach of his friend, and he turned and saw Kendal standing there. He looked disapproving.

'Shall we begin the proceedings?'

'Are you ready?' Briggs asked, somewhat mocking. As if his marriage was one on the time schedule of a man other than him.

His marriage that was not to be a marriage.

He looked at the lovely lines of the woman who would be his wife.

Not his wife in truth.

And then he looked back at Kendal. 'Yes. Let us hasten the imprisonment.'

Beatrice looked slightly wounded by that, but he did not see the purpose in soothing her. He was not going to be hard on her. Not in the end of all things. But he also did not see the purpose in making this any easier on her than it need be.

She had been the architect of this particular sort of destruction.

It does not matter to you.

It did not. It did not and would not matter to him. It could not.

The brothels would receive him whether or not he was newly wed.

And with thoughts of brothels lingering in his mind they entered the church again. The minister was standing there looking reproving, and Briggs had a strange sensation of guilt, which was not something he carried with him often. The minister must be very good.

Briggs could almost feel the hellfire against his heels as he stood there.

Sadly, he was a man who enjoyed the flames. He never had been properly able to feel shame.

Not over certain things.

He had been correct, the only other souls in attendance were Beatrice's mother, and Eleanor, the ward.

Eleanor, for her part, looked quite large-eyed and upset. On behalf of her friend no doubt. Being married off to the big bad Duke.

The minister read from the Book of Common Prayer, and Briggs's most dominant thought was how strange it was to be here again.

With yet another young, sweet miss.

But he was not the man that he'd been. Going into marriage with expectations of something entirely different.

He had been certain that he could make a friendship with his wife. At the very least.

Be something other than his parents' frosty union.

He had not managed it. If anything, he had failed.

He had failed at forging connections with all of the most important people in his life. With the exception of course of Kendal. Though that was likely somewhat compromised now.

It was a short ceremony. Quick and traditional. Legal. And that was all that mattered. They were married in the eyes of the church. And society would have to be appeased by the quick union.

It was incredible how decisive it was. A spare few words exchanged between two people who had been little more than acquaintances to each other a few days prior and they were now bound together for life.

And then they were bundled up into their carriage, making the three-hour journey to Maynard Park. And they had not exchanged a single word to each other since that moment in the garden.

'You will tell me, if you have need of anything,' he said.

'Such as?' she asked.

'Clothing. We are to go for the Season, I assume you will wish to go to... Balls.'

She blinked. 'I did not think that you would wish to attend them.'

'I do not,' he said. 'But you are my ward. Not my prisoner, for all that I may have alluded otherwise.'

'I'm not your ward,' she said softly.

'It is best if we think of it that way.'

And that he not think of last night, and the temptation he'd felt.

'I see.' She looked away from him. 'Well, I shall need

some dresses. It is not that my brother has not been generous, but this gown was taken from Eleanor. She had gowns made for the Season. I do not.'

'We shall remedy this.'

'Thank you.'

'It is nothing.'

'I cannot tell if you're angry with me,' she said. 'Am only I held to the standard of being perfectly honest, or does that apply to you as well?'

'Only you,' he said. She clearly did not see the amusement in this. 'It is for your protection,' he said further. 'I must know what you need, what you want, for if I do not, how can I care for you to the extent that you must be cared for?'

'How will I know anything if we do not speak with some level of honesty?'

'I imagine we shall continue on together as we began.'

'You are my brother's friend. We do not often speak. Occasionally, you have brought me sweets.'

'I do not see why that needs to change.'

She sighed. 'Well...should I call you Philip?'

Something rang out, sharp and hard in his chest. He did not know how many years it had been since he'd heard that name spoken out loud.

'No,' he said.

'We are married and...'

'Briggs will do just fine. When it is not Your Grace.' And how easy it was to imagine her calling him that from a position of supplication. On her knees.

Her pale breasts exposed completely...

He clenched his teeth.

'And you will call me...'

'Bea,' he said. 'Beatrice. As I always have. And I will bring you sweets and we can...'

'And I can go on as I ever was, but with a new lord and master? You rather than Hugh?'

He did not wish to think of being her lord and master.

It heated his blood. Brought back that image he'd had of her in that virginal nightgown. His sacrificial virgin.

His disgust with himself in that moment went so deep as to be in his bones.

Was he quite so perverse that even knowing how he'd disgusted Serena he could still desire to take Beatrice in hand this way?

There was a reason he consorted only with prostitutes.

'It is up to you, Beatrice, what you intend to make of this union.'

'No,' she said, 'it is not. It is not up to me, it is more up to my brother than it will ever be to me.'

'You were not to have a real marriage with your friend,' he said, looking at her and ignoring the crackling between them, and it was there. Real. Like a banked flame.

He did not like it.

'I know,' she said.

He knew why it was different. He did not have to ask.

'How old is your son?' she asked, sighing heavily, as if she'd accepted a subject change would be the only way to move forward.

He did not know why he didn't wish to speak of William with her.

She would be in the same residence as William in only a few hours. But he was... He was protective of the boy.

There were people who would not understand.

He wanted only to protect him from those who would...who would see his vulnerabilities and use them against him.

He did not wish for anyone to think unkindly of William. It was a fierce impulse, one that he could not quite make sense of. That, he supposed, was...being a father.

It was not the way his own had been. His own had seen his weaknesses and stabbed at them without mercy.

Had used them to devastate and torment.

'He is seven,' he said.

'I don't have any experience with children,' she said. 'I have always... I thought it should be nice to have my own.'

'I'm sorry for your disappointment.' He did mean it.

Being a father rooted him to the earth. Without William he wasn't sure what he would do. Spend his days and nights in brothels likely. Without a wife, a need to earn income or anyone on earth to answer to he would...

Stop trying.

He would sink into debauchery and obsession as deep as he could go and never surface.

William prevented that.

William was his reason for being a decent man. He had never felt a sense of pride or affection for his own father. He wanted William to feel both for him.

Whether or not he did was another matter.

'I should think it would be nice to have a child to care for,' she mused. 'In that way, I suppose you are preferable to James.'

'That is the only reason?' He looked at her, trying to ascertain if she truly did not have feelings for the man that went beyond friendship.

She'd said, but it seemed reasonable to him that she'd been harbouring finer feelings for him in some hidden chamber of her heart.

'No, he…he is easy and kind and I enjoy his company.'

'And I am…?' Briggs asked, because he could not help himself.

'You are occasionally kind when brandishing sweets, but no one would call you easy.'

He kicked his legs out forward and leaned back. 'Is that so?'

'You are too… You are you, Briggs, and I do not know how else to say it.'

'And James,' he said, ignoring that. 'Is he in love with you?'

'No,' she said. 'He…he has his reasons for wishing to marry me, but none of them include the kind of love you mean.'

There were not many reasons that a man would wish to enter into a sham marriage, but Briggs could think of one quite obvious reason. He wished for her sake she could have married her friend. They could've likely had a companionable union.

More's the pity for all involved.

'I do not know what I'm supposed to feel,' she said. 'For I am a married woman now, but not a married woman. And I am angry, because I think there are many mysteries in the world that will be withheld from me because of this. Because you are intent on treating me as a ward and not a wife.'

She was edging into dangerous territory, and he knew that she had no real knowledge of that. No real concept.

It had always been thus with her. She was forceful in her speech and he often wondered if it was due to how she had been treated in her illness. As if she was trying to prove she was not fragile.

'There are some mysteries that you might find are best left that way.'

'So you say,' she prodded, her cheeks turning a deep shade of rose. From embarrassment or anger he could not say. Though he was nearly certain it was both. 'Because you are a man and nothing is barred from you. I cannot tell you how infuriating it has been to attempt to divine how to orchestrate my own ruin when I am not entirely certain what it is that ruins a woman. It is being found alone with a man certainly. And being in your embrace. But I do not know what further there is to such an embrace. Or children. I am aware that one must be married to have children. But I'm not aware of what occurs to make it so. Clearly it is something beyond vows, or my brother would not have been so quick to allow me to marry you, no matter how tenuous a state my reputation was in.'

'I will provide you with reading material,' he said. He had no intention of doing such a thing. If she wished to comb through his library…

Of course, his library contained reading material of a more graphic nature, rather than informational.

'You are infuriating. The whole of mankind is infuriating.'

He chuckled. 'Oh, I do not disagree with you.'

She leaned back in the seat across from him, and he found he could not take his eyes off her. Her skin was light cream, her curves so much more ample than he had realised. There was something sweet and sulky about her mouth. He had never noticed that before. And the way that she looked at him. It was a particular sort of look. Demure, when he knew she was not. Not really.

She straightened, and her eyes sharpened. He did not like it. 'We have all this time. Why not give me an education yourself, rather than referring me to your library?'

And those words hit him with the strength of a gunpowder keg going off.

He knew she did not mean to be provocative, for she did not even understand provocation. Did not know why a woman had to take care not to rouse a man's appetites. Did not understand why men and women could not be alone together without a chaperon.

Truly.

She was appallingly uninformed. And somehow, was managing to inflame him almost more because of it.

'You've spent most of your life in the country,' he said.

'Yes.'

He would regret this. But she was his now. That made a strange sensation crystallise inside him.

A lock turning in a key.

She was his. Under his care. And he would care for her. She would have the finest of gowns. He would ensure that she wanted for nothing. She would be happier with him. Happier than she had been back at Bybee House.

And as she belonged to him, it was his decision just how in depth her education was or was not. She wanted freedom. She was a married woman now, whether or not they ever consummated that union.

He locked his jaw together at the thought.

Beatrice.

She was beautiful. But there was much more to sex than beauty.

Many women were beautiful.

He preferred his beauties bought and paid for. A transaction that required no exchange of self, just bodies.

Yes, Beatrice was beautiful, but that did not mean he could not control himself with her.

He had always *liked* Beatrice. Had always felt a measure of pity for her, to be sure. She had been a cloistered girl, and when he'd first met her she had never ventured out of the family drawing room.

'What have you seen of animals?'

Dear God, he was pushing things where he ought not. And yet, the realisation did not stop him.

Impulse control had always been a problem.

Unless he was with a woman or focused on his orchids. Both were singular pursuits that required an intensity of focus he otherwise found impossible.

'Animals?'

'Have you never seen animals engaged in…procreation?'

She blinked. Rapidly. 'No,' she said.

He was counting on that. He was counting on an amorous hedgehog to have made this easier for him.

Currently, he felt enraged with the whole of the species.

'Never mind.'

'I was kept inside most of my childhood. Yes, I did grow up in the country. But in truth, I mostly grew up *in* Bybee House. I spent a great deal of my childhood in bed in my room.'

An orchid.

The thought bloomed in his head and took root.

Beautiful. Fragile.

Needing a firm, guiding hand.

He gritted his teeth. 'What were your ailments?'

He had never truly discussed this with Kendal, as it was not his concern. Or, hadn't been before. 'I need to know,' he said. 'I need to know, so that I understand how best to care for you.'

'I have been just fine these many years, Your Grace.'

'You are in my care,' he said. 'And that matters to me. I take care of what is mine.'

'I do not…belong to you.'

'The Church of England would see it differently.'

'My breathing. My throat would become very tight, and it would become nearly impossible to take a breath. And any illness of the lungs always… Progressed. Badly. I would get very hot and… They would have to bleed me.'

'And now?'

'It is not so frequent. I have not had a true attack of it in years.'

'That is a terrible way to spend a childhood,' he said.

'I learned to find ways to appreciate it,' she said, her expression deathly serious and hard as stone. 'I hated the bleeding at first. But I would imagine that it was making me stronger. That it was draining away the bad, and that the pain was fortifying me in some way.' She got a strange, faraway look in her eyes. 'And I remember the first time I escaped from the house. And I exerted myself in ways I was not permitted to. I ran through a field. My breathing did become quite hard, but I hid it. I enjoyed it, even. For it was a mark of freedom. And while I was running I fell. But the pain that I felt then was the most real thing. The ground biting into my skin. It was my consequence. Mine. And it was… Somehow wonderful.'

He felt frozen in the moment, not because he was uncertain, no. In these matters Briggs did not traffic in uncertainty.

No, he wanted to stop and linger in it. In the spark it ignited beneath his skin.

The way she spoke of pain. As if it transformed her. Gave her power.

He knew that feeling. He was not the one who received, but the one who gave. The feeling of absolute control—so unlike how he'd always felt otherwise.

The world had felt wrong for him. Everything in it insensible. He'd had little control over his moods. He'd found solace in his obsession with botany, then in growing flowers himself. Cultivating something with his hands that was both delicate and difficult.

When he'd got older he'd begun to fantasise about women. Controlling their pleasure in the way he controlled the bloom of an orchid.

He had never considered that Beatrice might be the one who understood, but there she was, explaining the piece of pain she experienced in a way not even he had ever heard.

And he was held transfixed.

Of the strange expression on her face, and of the deep, yawning hunger that he could feel it open up inside him.

'And your breathing now?' he asked, doing his best to move past this moment. 'How is it?'

'Mostly manageable. I rarely have incidents now.

I have not been sick for many years. The doctor does fear that my lungs are weak. Because of that he feels… carrying a child, giving birth…is something I likely cannot survive. That is why. My lungs.'

'And your susceptibility to other illnesses, I imagine.'

'Yes,' she said, her voice sounding distant. 'I imagine.'

'And that is why you've never seen hedgehogs rut,' he said.

She wrinkled her nose. '*Rut*. That does not sound pleasant.'

'It is not. To watch hedgehogs do it.'

He was walking a thin line. And he knew it.

Like when he'd held her to him last night.

'It is oversimplified,' he said. 'To reduce it all to the creation of the child.'

'But they are connected,' she said, pressing. 'That does make me feel better as it makes me sense that there are perhaps *less* things that I do not know about.'

She had no idea.

'Or so much *more*,' he said.

'That is *not* cheering.'

'You may find none of this cheering in the end. Have you ever kissed a man?' He sensed that she had not.

'No,' she said, her cheeks turning pink.

'Not your friend James?'

She looked away. 'I told him I was not in love with him.'

'Love does not always matter when it comes to issues of attraction, I'm afraid.'

'All of this is confusing.'

'It is,' he said. 'Sometimes deliciously so. There are times when you want a person you may despise. When you might want someone who is utterly forbidden to you.' *Treading on the line now, Briggs.* 'Does he make you feel warm?'

Her eyes went round. 'Warm?'

He cursed himself even as he moved to the seat beside her in the carriage. 'When he is close to you,' he said, lowering his voice. 'Do you feel warm? Flushed?'

She drew back, her eyes getting wide. 'No.'

He was meanly satisfied by that. 'He is your friend, then.'

'I said,' she responded, her voice breathless.

And it was not fair. For he was a terrible rake and he was pressing the limits of it here with her, and of his own self-control.

Were his tastes in shagging more mainstream he would be an even more incorrigible one. As it was, he had to be selective about his partners. He knew how to make a woman want him. He could make her understand. But what was the purpose of it? What was the purpose when…? This was not what he had been tasked with. Not at all.

'I feel warm sometimes when you're near me,' she said.

Dammit.

'Now?' he asked.

'Always,' she whispered, as if it were a revelation.

And he tried not to think of when he'd had a handful of her buttock. How round and supple it was. How perfectly it fitted his palm.

How she'd felt leaning against him on the swing.

How that dress lovingly showed the curve of her bosom.

'If I were to kiss you,' he said. 'It would increase. Quite exponentially. And you would understand. You would want to be closer to me. I to you. And it would feel the most natural thing in all the world to remove anything that stood between us.'

'I don't...'

'Clothes.' He was torturing himself, and he could not say why.

He preferred to mete out pain, not be on the receiving end of it.

'I *knew* that naked nymphs had something to do with it,' she said, looking up at him, as if in a daze.

'Naked nymphs?'

'I saw a book. In my father's library. In his collection. There were...' Her cheeks turned pink. 'Naked women. Nymphs. Running from men.'

He bit his own tongue. To remind himself why he needed control. 'Yes. They were running to preserve their virtue, I have a feeling. For if the men caught them, had their way with them...'

'You speak in more veiled metaphor. *Have their way with them.* I wish to understand. What it means.'

'You are familiar with the ways in which men and women are different?'

His wife had been given a basic bit of education from her own mother before they wed. He had not had to explain everything to her. Beatrice... Beatrice would have to have everything explained to her were they to have a true wedding night. And they were not.

But he had always liked to tease flames. He didn't know why he was suddenly taking the torture, rather than giving it.

Though, Beatrice was not untortured.

'I have seen anatomy,' she said, sniffing. 'Drawings. In science books. And, of course...statuary.'

Ah, the naked limp statuary. Which would give her no real idea of men at all. At least, not of him.

She does not need an idea of you.

'The purpose of the difference is that we fit together,' he said. 'And that is the way in which you create a child. But it is more than that. It can be much more than that.'

Her eyes rounded, her lips going slack. 'What more?'

She sounded dazed, and she sounded fascinated, and he truly wished she were neither.

'Pleasure.' He looked at her, and he did not break her gaze. 'Pain. Which for some is quite near to the same thing.'

Her blue eyes glistened with something then, a keen interest he wished to turn away from. But could not. 'Is it?'

'Yes.'

'Briggs...'

They were saved by the fact that the carriage arrived at Maynard Park. He did not much believe in divine intervention, but he was going to have to give serious consideration to it at this moment.

The old place was grand, he had to admit, but he had no real fond feelings for it. He had not had the happiest of childhoods, and then he had not had the happiest of beginnings as a man. He'd had the interior renewed, and had ensured the gardens were revamped as well, and had seen to the installation of a greenhouse.

It didn't completely erase the memories of what it had been like to grow up here.

And you keep your son there. Locked up like the prisoner you once were.

He pushed that thought away.

It was different.

The driver manoeuvred the carriage to the front of the grand entrance hall. It was all stately pillars in marble. Not to his taste. And yet it was his. And it felt in many ways as if it spoke to a great many things that he was. A great many of the wrong things.

He assisted his wife from the carriage, unwilling to allow the footman to place a finger on her. His possessiveness was unfamiliar. He was accustomed to it in the context of an interlude with a woman. After all, that was a hallmark of the dynamic. But he was not accustomed to it when he was fully clothed. And he wondered... He wondered if he might find a strange sort of fulfilment from this. From caring for her. Having her.

Even if only in this regard.

He escorted her to the front of the house, and the door opened, his butler a firm and imposing presence.

Mrs Brown the housekeeper was standing just there, smiling warmly. 'Your Grace,' she said. And she made her way to Beatrice and clasped her hand. 'Your Grace.'

'Hello,' Beatrice said, suddenly looking awestruck and shy.

'Do not worry,' he said.

And he could feel her calm next to him.

'I am Mrs Brown. I'm the housekeeper.'

'I'm pleased to meet you,' Beatrice said.

And then he heard a great howl echoing through the halls. Beatrice startled.

'No need for alarm,' Mrs Brown said, smiling. 'It is only that he's having to change for dinner. He did not wish to stop what he was doing.'

'William,' he said. 'That's my son.'

'Is he well?'

'Yes,' Mrs Brown said. 'He is quite all right. I assure you.'

But there was something worried behind her eyes, and he hated to see that.

As much as this…discontentment in his son chafed against something inside him.

'Welcome to Maynard Park.'

Chapter Six

Beatrice woke up, her heart thundering. It took her several moments to realise where she was. She was in Briggs's house. She was Briggs's wife.

She was sleeping alone. In an unfamiliar bedchamber. And she could hear a sound that was like howling.

She turned over and put her pillow over her head, trying to drown out the haunting sound, sleep tangling with reality until she was on the moors running from a ghost, rather than safe beneath the bedclothes.

When she woke her eyes felt swollen and she felt gritty and bruised.

She took breakfast in the morning room, and did not see Briggs.

She had a small meeting with Mrs Brown, standing in the hall nearest the entry, and made arrangements to plan the menu for the week.

Beatrice had to admit she found that cheering, and hoped that she found the food at Maynard to be to her liking. It was not as if she was fussy, but she enjoyed nice foods rather a lot.

Her pleasures in life had been small, always, but very deeply enjoyed.

She went into the library and found a copy of *Emma*, which she had read before but had quite enjoyed. She tucked it under her arm and there was an attractive illustrated compendium of birds, and she added that too.

She took them back to her room and looked around the space. It was elegant, the walls a blue silk, with matching blue silk on the bed, trimmed with gold. The ornate canopy had heavy curtains, though she couldn't see why she should need to draw curtains back in this isolated room that only ever contained herself or her maid.

She deposited the books at the foot of her bed and went back out into the hall.

And that was when she saw him for the first time.

The boy.

He had unruly brown hair and slim shoulders. He was very slight, his expression sulky.

William.

This must be William.

The boy turned and went back down the hall. Towards the sound of the late-night howling, she realised.

Over the next few days she spotted the boy in the house a few times, but never Briggs, who seemed to ensconce himself in his study at the early morning and not…un-ensconce himself until well after she was ready to retire for the evening.

And sometimes at night, she heard that howling.

One word came to her each time she saw that child.

Loneliness.

She knew it well. She was living it now.

When she crawled into bed on her fourth night at Maynard, her fourth night as a wife, she tried to read *Emma*. And could not.

Because in those words she looked for any…anything she might be able to recognise. Longings, feelings. She could not…find herself in those pages.

Briggs did not want her. Not really. He did not care if she was here or at Bybee House.

She felt no giddy joy over marriage and could not care at all about the marital prospects of the silly girls in the novel.

She set it aside and stared at the ornate ceiling of the canopy, her eyes tracing the lines of the gold crest there.

Was this to be her life? Not any better or altered than that life at Bybee House?

No. She would…she would not allow it.

And that was when the howling started.

She got up from the bed without thinking and raced to the door. She cracked it open and held herself still there, waiting. The howling grew louder. And she walked out of the room, making her way down the cavernous hall. It was a huge home. Not unlike Bybee House. Though less Grecian in style. She had noted the frescoes painted on the walls; they were a bit more vivid than the ones to be found there.

But it wasn't the frescoes that had her full attention now. It was that sound. Like a wounded animal.

William. She knew it was William.

She raced towards it, not thinking. And pushed the door open. It was another bedchamber. A child's room. And the child was on the floor, dressed in his bed clothes, weeping and thrashing.

He had not met her, not yet. They had only seen

each other from a distance, and she hesitated to make a move, for she would be a stranger to him. But no one else was here.

So she raced towards him and dropped to her knees. 'William,' she said.

But he said nothing in response. He only kept screaming and crying, twisting to get away from her. It took her a moment to realise that he was sleeping. Sleeping, and lost to reason. Lost to any sort of reach.

'William,' she said softly, reaching her hand towards him, her heart contracting painfully.

She had never experienced anything like this. But when she was a child her body had been in agony sometimes. And she had felt as if no one in the room could truly reach her. As if she was living in her own space, where there was only pain. And she had learned to place herself there firmly, to find a way to endure it. But it was always lonely. There was never connection there. There was never a space to be comforted.

There was only enduring.

And she broke, for this boy. For this boy who was experiencing that now.

This boy she saw alone.

She lurched forward, just as he retreated to the wall, hitting himself against it. She grabbed hold of him and pulled him against her body, holding his arms down, holding him still.

'Be still,' she said, making a shushing noise. 'Be still.' She held on to him tightly. 'You are well. You are safe.'

It took a time, but eventually the screams quieted. Eventually, he surrendered to the way that she held him.

He was not alone now.

'Be at peace, William,' she whispered.

Silence descended, finally. He was damp with sweat and breathing hard, his exhaustion palpable.

She held him against her breast, swaying back and forth, some instinct guiding her.

The door opened, and she could see it was Mrs Brown.

'Your Grace,' she said. 'I apologise. You should not have been disturbed. It took me a wee while to rouse myself…'

'Does this happen often?' she asked, already knowing it did, for this was not the first time she'd heard him.

'Yes. He has nightmares.'

'I have heard him…upset like this during the day as well.'

'It is not the same. He is easily…angered by changes in his routine.'

'I see.'

'This should not have fallen to you. It is my responsibility to see to him at night. His governess needs rest. She is in a room far from him for that reason, after her day she is tired.'

'I do not mind,' she said.

'Often, when he is here, His Grace sees to him. He must be in his study still.'

As far as she could tell, His Grace was only ever in his study.

She was relieved to hear he did see to his son. She had yet to see the two of them together.

'It is all right,' she said, stroking the boy's head. She picked him up, his form limp. And she returned him to his bed. 'Does he usually sleep after this?'

'Yes. There may be another episode, but typically one is all he will have on a difficult night.'

'I'm glad to hear that. But I will listen for him.'

'If you insist, Your Grace,' Mrs Brown said, clearly at her limit with how much she was willing to argue with the new Duchess.

'Yes.'

She was filled with a sense of purpose. For she had comforted the boy. And she could comfort the boy. She might not ever be a wife to Briggs, not truly. But she could be a mother to this boy. Because she had understood him in that moment. It might be an entirely different circumstance, and entirely different…everything, but she understood. On a deep, profound level. For he lived in a space that people could not reach him in, and she had spent much of her childhood doing the same.

Being ill. Being shut up inside.

Tonight had been like witnessing a person who was shut up inside themselves. She knew what that was like as well.

As she had said. A spirit that was held back by the body she was in.

She waited a while, and then she returned to her room, her heart rate slowing. And as she drifted off to sleep, she made a plan. A plan for the next day. She would not simply be a ward. She was going to take charge of her life. She was going to find out what she could do. What she wanted.

And she would begin with William.

The next morning at breakfast time, she went in search of the child.

She found him in the nursery with his governess, sitting at a small table and looking furious.

'William…' The woman was saying his name in a cajoling manner.

'Good morning,' Beatrice said, coming into the room.

The boy did not look at her. 'William,' she said, saying his name purposefully. 'Good morning.'

He looked up in her direction. Though his eyes did not meet hers. 'Hello,' he said.

'You had a difficult sleep last night,' she said.

His expression went black and he turned his head away. 'Who are you?'

'Did your father speak to you about the fact he was getting married?'

The boy did not answer.

'Did your father tell you that he was getting married?' She restated the question.

The boy nodded, his head still angled away from her.

'I'm his wife. I am your stepmother. You may call me Beatrice,' she said.

He lowered his head, his focus back on his breakfast.

Beatrice moved to him, and sat down. He looked up, startled by her presence. His eyes connected with hers for a moment before darting away. It was as if it was difficult for him to look straight at her.

'I like to swing,' she said, feeling as if there had to be a way to capture his interest. 'I like to read. And I like to hide in the garden. What do you like?'

He didn't say a thing. But he stood up and went to his bedside table and opened a drawer, pulling out a small box. He opened it and held it out to her.

Inside was a small collection of cards, with pictures on them.

'This is the Colosseum,' he said. 'It is in Rome. It

was inaugurated in AD 80. This is the Pantheon,' he said, showing her the next card.

He continued showing her sites from all over Europe, with a special focus on those found in Italy. His knowledge was breathtaking. He knew dates and locations, precise details. And he seemed perfectly happy to give her each and every one.

'Do you wish to go to these places?' she asked.

'Yes,' the boy answered.

'So, this is a box of your dreams,' she said, smiling.

His brow creased. 'It is a box of cards.'

He looked so like his father then. And the realisation sent a strange sort of twist through Beatrice's midsection. He was part of Briggs. It was undeniable. She could see it so clearly now.

'Well, they are very nice cards,' she said.

She sat with the boy, who said nothing more voluntarily throughout his breakfast. His governess stood in the corner, watching her with hard interest. It was not entirely accepting, but she had a feeling that the woman was protective of the boy. Beatrice herself had no real experience with children, so she did not know what she should expect of the child. He seemed different, though. That much she knew.

She wondered if she did. For she had certainly not spent much time in the company of those who were not her family. She had her few very close friends, and that was all. She did not spend time out in broader society.

'William,' she said. 'I should like to see the grounds today. Remember how I told you I like gardens?'

'To hide,' he said.

'Yes. But, also to walk in them. Is there a spot in the garden here that you favour best?'

'No,' he said.

'I see.' She tried to think of another way to say it. 'Is there a place that is interesting? Where you can tell me about the flowers?'

Something in his expression changed. 'Yes. There is a garden and it has statues. I like that spot best. It reminds me of Rome.'

'Excellent. Shall you and I take a picnic for our lunch this afternoon?'

'I do not eat outside,' he said.

'Well, perhaps you might try?'

'I do not eat outside.'

'Should you like to eat outside?'

'I don't know.'

'All right. Then we shall try it. And if you don't like it, we don't have to do it.'

He looked thoughtful about this. 'All right.'

'Then you and I shall see each other this afternoon.'

She stood and walked out of the nursery, and heard the footsteps of his governess behind.

'Master William does not like interruptions to his schedule,' she said.

'No, I imagine he does not. But I would like to begin a new schedule. I would like to spend time with him.'

Beatrice had no experience of running a household, but she had watched her brother and her mother do it in decent fashion for a number of years. She did not feel fully confident in her position, but one thing she did feel confident in was her connection to the boy. It was loneliness. It echoed inside her, and she knew that it echoed inside him as well. She knew that he felt the same sort of isolation that she did. It did not matter if they were the same, or different, those feelings she knew.

And she would not rattle around this house doing nothing. She could not do that.

'Perhaps we should speak to His Grace.'

'You are welcome to speak to His Grace,' Beatrice said. 'I am not sure where he is. I am not sure what his routine is. I only know that I must make my own. And I should like it to include William.'

The governess was wary. 'William can be a difficult child,' she said.

'I'm continually warned of this,' she said. 'I held him last night when he was overtaken by terror in his sleep. I understand. When I arrived he was quite upset. But I do not think that makes him difficult.'

'I love him,' his governess said. 'That is not what I mean.'

'I believe you,' she said. 'And I wish for you to believe me. I do not wish to toy with this child. But I have married His Grace, and I… I must find a reason to be here.' She had not meant to say that. Had not meant to expose herself in such a fashion. Or their marriage. For it was nobody's business that it was not a true union.

Though they had forgone the traditional honeymoon trip. And indeed any sort of honeymoon phase.

She did not know how they might express that, but she had a feeling it was not as they had been these past days.

'I want to be a mother to this boy.'

'Forgive me, Your Grace,' the governess said. 'His own mother did not care for him, and I am quite protective.'

Her stomach went tight. 'My father did not care for me,' she said. 'I was blessed to have a wonderful mother, however. But even so, I know what it is to have a parent who does not care. And to lose that parent quite early. I do not wish to cause him harm. And I promise you that should he become upset, I will bring him to you.'

'Thank you, Your Grace. What am I to do with my time?'

'Whatever you wish,' Beatrice said. 'Take some time to rest. Or read.'

'Oh, I don't...'

'Do not worry.'

Beatrice went to the kitchen and asked about having a picnic compiled for herself and Master William. She was met with slightly quizzical expressions, but nobody openly questioned her. And she spent the next hour considering what she might wear out in the garden.

While she was being dressed, she took a moment to ponder the absurdity of it all.

She had been a spectator in her own life for a great many years. Subject to the commands or the whims of those in authority over her. Even if they did love her. And here she was, taking part in running a household, caring for a child. She was deeply surprised and pleased by all of it and she might be confused about everything with Briggs, but it didn't matter. She had not had any of this a week ago. Not this home, not this child. Not the sense of purpose. Husband was inconsequential. And she did not have unlimited freedom, it was true. But she had more freedom. Or rather... A different sort of freedom. A different sort of life. It might not be an adventure around Europe, no grand tour. But she had taken a small one sitting on the floor with William this morning.

And it was not mouldering away in the country. Well, she supposed she was mouldering away in the country, but it was a different part of the country. So, there was that to be cheerful about.

In the end, she was deeply satisfied by the blue dress that her lady's maid put her in. It was a light airy fabric, and she attired herself in a fichu to cover the swells of her bosom. It was not ballroom, after all.

But she looked... Entirely like the Duchess of the house, and not like the child she had felt like only a week before. She was a woman. As close to making her own decisions as she possibly could be, at least, to the best of her knowledge.

Time had passed quickly, and before she knew it was time to collect William.

The boy that she found stubbornly sitting in the corner of his room, was not quite the amiable chap she had met this morning.

His dark head was lowered, and his face was fixed into a comical scowl. He had dark-looking circles under his eyes.

'Are you tired?' she asked.

'No,' he said.

'He has had a bit of difficulty with lessons today.'

'I sometimes had difficulty with lessons too,' she said, trying her best to relate to him. She reached down, and tried to take hold of his hand, but he would not rise, and instead, leaned backwards, rooting himself even more firmly to the ground.

'William, I have very nice food in this basket.'

He did not say anything.

'Shall we put your shoes on?'

'No,' he said.

'And why not?'

'I don't want them.'

'You must have shoes.'

He only lay down on the floor, not answering her at all.

'I will see to him, Your Grace,' the governess said.

'No,' Beatrice said, confused, but determined. 'William,' she said, trying to sound stout. 'I'm going to have a picnic. I will have one here if I must. But I am intent upon eating with you.'

He rolled to the side, not looking at her.

She took the blanket that was draped over her arm and spread it out over the floor of the nursery. Right atop the beautiful rug. Then she sat determinedly, placing the basket beside her and beginning to place the food all around them. 'I am quite hungry.'

'No,' he said.

'Well I am.'

'I don't like it. I don't want shoes.'

'If we eat here you don't have to put on shoes.'

'I don't want shoes,' he said.

'I said you did not have to have them.'

'I do not want shoes.'

She did not know what to make of it. He seemed upset, though not inconsolable. He made his statement about shoes at least four more times before going quiet. As if the idea was firmly rooted in his mind and he required extra time to ensure it had been dealt with.

Beatrice decided to change her tactics.

'Do you like cheese?'

The boy did not answer. He was involved in examining a spot on the wallpaper.

'I quite like it,' she said, firmly, cheerfully.

She stared at him for a moment and wondered if she had miscalculated, in a fit of arrogance, imagining that she understood him. His loneliness seemed to be something he chose. For he did not look at her. And he did not seem interested in her overtures.

But maybe he simply didn't know how.

'William, do you know it is polite to look at someone when they are talking?'

He turned his head, sharply and only for a moment. And then he went back to staring at the wall. 'I don't like it.'

'You don't like to look at people?'

'No.'

She searched herself, trying to sort out the best way forward. 'What do you like to look at?'

'I already showed you my cards.'

'You did.'

For her part, she ate some cheese, because it made her feel soothed.

She heard heavy footsteps coming down the hall, and stilled. It could be a manservant, but it made her think of...

The door pushed open, and there he was.

His eyes connected with hers, and he looked momentarily surprised. And then... Angry.

'What are you doing in here?' he asked.

She expected William to scramble upwards at his father's presence. But he did not. Instead, he remained as he was, laying with his back to her, facing the wall.

'I'm having a picnic with William,' she said, smiling determinedly. 'Would you like to join us, Your Grace?'

He frowned. Which was a feat as he'd been frowning already, but he managed to do it again. 'Would I care to join you…in a picnic?'

'Yes,' she said brightly. 'I have not seen you these many days.'

She looked at William, who was kicking his feet idly, but still not looking.

'Good afternoon, William,' Briggs said. 'How are you?'

He didn't respond to his father.

Briggs, for his part, did not look perturbed by this at all.

'Don't you want to say hello to your father?' Beatrice prompted.

'It is no matter,' Briggs said. 'Sometimes William does not feel like saying hello.'

She was surprised by the easy way that he accepted this.

Confused, she shuffled over, making more room on the blanket. 'You want to join us. Surely you've not taken your lunch yet?'

'I have not. But I do not sit on the ground.'

'That is very interesting as William informed me earlier that he does not eat outside.' She adjusted her seating position on the floor and it made her dress go tight around her hips, which caught his attention more than it should.

'And you told him what?'

'I asked him to try.' She looked like steel just then.

His brows lifted. 'And here you are, eating indoors.'

'Far easier to accomplish than the moving of a large dining table up to this room, don't you think?'

'You think that you will win with me where you have not won with my son?'

'Yes,' she said.

'Have a picnic.' It was William's first acknowledgement of Briggs.

They both stared at the child. Who looked serious.

'Have a picnic,' he repeated.

'There,' she said, smiling up at Briggs. 'William wishes you to have a picnic.'

Chapter Seven

Briggs was… He didn't know what he was. Of all the things he had expected when he had walked into his son's room, it had not been to see Beatrice sitting with a determinedly cheerful expression on her face in the middle of a blanket on the floor, eating a picnic.

Nor did he expect to see William laying on his side, staring at the wall.

Beatrice might interpret this as insolence, but Briggs knew that it was not. He also knew that if William were unhappy with Beatrice's presence, he would've made it known. He would not simply lie there quietly.

He had been avoiding her.

That was the truth. And now that he acknowledged it to himself he felt replete with cowardice, and cowardice was not something he trafficked in. He had told himself that it was for her own good. After all, the conversation in the carriage ride had steered far too close to intimate for what he had decided their marriage would be. But he had also decided that she was his. And he fundamentally could not excuse his neglect of her. Not when her care and keeping was his responsibility.

What he had not expected was for her to be with William. And he felt... Oddly exposed, and angry about it. At war with the emotions that Beatrice created inside him.

And he found himself sitting down. On the floor. He hated that she was right. But he could not deny William. And he had asked him to have a picnic.

'William has shown me his collection of cards.'

'Has he?'

'Yes. I quite enjoyed hearing about everything he knows.'

'Unless you've spent a considerable amount of hours with him, you have not scratched the surface of what he knows,' Briggs said, marvelling slightly at the pride that he felt when he said it. William was in possession of a great deal of information. And while he might not be able to carry on a fluid conversation about whatever you wanted him to, he could certainly give you all of the information there was to have on the Roman Colosseum.

'I don't doubt that,' Beatrice said.

William rolled over then, as if he was intrigued by the direction of the conversation. Briggs couldn't help but smile.

'You know quite a lot, don't you, William?'

'I know everything about the Colosseum,' William said.

'William, are you interested in London?'

'London is interesting,' he said. 'Westminster and St James's Palace.'

'You're very clever,' she said. 'Do you look forward to joining us in London?'

'He won't be joining us,' Briggs said.

William did not react to that.

'Why not?' Beatrice asked.

'He will not be joining us because he does not like to travel. He finds carriage rides to be interminable, and the disruption to his routine makes him fractious.'

'Oh, it all makes me fractious as well,' Beatrice said. 'I am quite upended, and a bit fussy. But that does not mean we should not do things.'

'He will not wish to go to London.'

'London has Westminster Abbey, St James's Palace. Grosvenor Square.'

He recited facts rather than stating his feelings on the matter, and that did not surprise Briggs. Sometimes he seemed to be making a conversation, and other times, you couldn't force one out of him. Briggs didn't see the point in trying.

He let him speak his piece, though.

But he found that he did not necessarily want Beatrice to see, for he was afraid on behalf of William that she would offer judgement, but she did not.

'You should've spoken to me, before you involved yourself with William.'

'She is my friend,' William said.

Briggs was absolutely stunned by that. He did not know what to say. 'She is?'

'I've never had a friend,' he said.

'You have your governess.'

'She is a governess. This lady is my friend.'

'I cannot argue with that.'

Beatrice, for her part, looked exceedingly pleased.

They continued eating in silence, and when they were through, William's governess came and made it clear that it was time for him to continue on with his lessons.

They walked out of the nursery, and Beatrice left behind him.

'Why can we not take him to London?'

'Why have you inserted yourself into my son's life?' he asked.

'I had nothing else to do,' she said. 'I felt that I had something in common with Master William. I am lonely. And I can assure you that he is as well.'

'Did he look lonely to you?' His son barely glanced at people when they were in the same room as he, not when he was engrossed in something else.

'I somehow have the feeling that he does not necessarily look the way you or I might when we are feeling something. But it does not mean he does not feel it.'

He was stunned by the insight, as he had known that was true for some time. Even if no one, including William himself, could confirm it.

'You are correct about that, but that does not mean that he is lonely. Or that he wishes to go to London. You have spent some time with him, and that is very nice of you. A kindness. However, that does not give you a complete view of all of his struggles.'

'I went into his room last night. When he was having one of his terrors.'

Guilt ate at him. He ought to have heard William, but he had been in his study. He had spent much time there since bringing Beatrice to Maynard Park. Anything to keep her distant from him in the night when his vision was invaded by thoughts of beautiful virgin sacrifices, on their knees before him...

'Yes, that is one of his difficulties. He sometimes does that during the day as well, though, when he is not asleep. His moods can be incredibly capricious. I

do not always know what will cause… There is a dis-
connect. He loses himself. In his rage. He has never
harmed anyone. I do not think he ever would. I cannot
explain it better than that. But I do not think he would
enjoy London. I think you would find it noisy, I think
you would find it confusing, I think you would find
the journey arduous. And I am his father. You might
think that I have made this edict out of a sense of my
own convenience, but I assure you it is not for my convenience. It is not so simple. Would that it were for my
own convenience. Then I might not feel so much guilt.
I might not feel torn. By my duties to him, and my duties to the House of Lords.'

He felt a stab of guilt, because there was also the duty
to his libido, which he had faithfully attended these past
years. But that was part of quitting to London. At least
for him. The opportunity to see to his baser needs. And
he had a great need to deal with them now.

Of course, he would already have Beatrice in tow.

Beatrice likely had no idea what a brothel was, let
alone the particular delights he saw in them.

She looked at him in a fury. 'Your Grace, I did not
seek to question your commitment to your son, but I do
have a differing opinion. He dreams of seeing things.
He dreams of seeing the world. I think perhaps in part
the trip will be upsetting for him, but it seems as if you
find sleep upsetting at times, and he cannot be utterly
and completely shielded from every bad feeling.'

'Why not? Why do you think that is not something
that should be done? You had the benefit of having it
done for you. And you discarded it. You discarded your
brother's protection, and now you are under mine. And
you must do as I say.'

He had not asked for this. For her intervention with his son, his most private, painful relationship. The one he would die for, kill for.

He had not asked for her to be here, bewitching him and making him long to touch her. Taste her.

Receive her submission.

This was her fault, and not his.

If she did not like the way it was in his household, she should not have flung herself into his arms.

'Is that how it's to be, Your Grace?'

'And when is it that I became Your Grace, and not Briggs?'

'The moment you stopped being my friend. Maybe you never started. I believed that we were friends, Your Grace, I did. I had a great deal of affection for you. But since all of this, all you have done is stay in your study.'

'This is what I do with my life, Beatrice. You have always seen me when I was away from my duties and responsibilities. You only ever see me away from Maynard Park. *This* is my life. I have a duty to my tenants to manage things to the best of my ability. I have a son, and my duty is to make sure that his life… I wish for him to be happy, Beatrice, and I do not know how to accomplish this. There is no road map. There is no map for parents, not in the general sense, but when you have a child like mine, who is not like any other child I have ever met, how is it that I'm supposed to ensure his happiness? When cards with pictures of buildings on them make him happier than toys, and when he does not always smile even when he is happy. How am I to ever know what to do?

'Do not speak to me with such authority and confidence. Do not tell me what I have denied you, when you are the one that put yourself in the situation. You wanted my anger, and now you may have it. You might have got your way. You might have escaped from your house, but you have stepped into my life. And I warned you that I would not disrupt it for you.'

She looked wounded, and he regretted it. But she had no right to speak to him on such matters. She might be a woman in figure, but she was a child in so many ways. Desperately sheltered.

'I was a child like that. It might not have been for the same reasons,' she said, her voice filled with conviction, 'but I was that child. My parents did not know what to do. Hugh has never known what to do with me. I have been isolated and alone because of the differences in me. Because of the fear that my family has always felt for me. And it might come from a place of love, but the result is the same. I have been lonely. And isolated. Controlled. And at the same time… Do you know what it is to be a child who has accepted that you will likely die? Because all of that fear that surrounded me all the time, I knew what it meant. I knew that it meant I was dying. I was surprised to wake up some days. Many days. I endured pain that would make grown men weep. And I learned to do so without fear. Having a different set of circumstances does not make you weak. I am not weak. Your son is not weak.'

'I did not say that either of you was weak.'

'When you deny him the chance to fail, it reveals that is what you think.'

'Beatrice, you have spent your life cloistered in the house. You do not have a child. You do not know what I have endured, what it has cost me to try to be the best father that I can be to him.'

'I do not deny it,' she said. 'I am certain that you have...endured a great many difficult and painful things trying to parent him, but that does not... Maybe it is helpful for me to challenge you.'

'You have spent a few hours of my son, you do not know him.' And he felt guilt. Because he was not listening to her. And he did know it.

He was denying the strength he knew was in her, choosing instead to focus on her weakness, which was a petty and small thing to do.

But he had not asked for Beatrice to uproot his life, any more than he had asked for any of this. What he had done, he had done for her.

For her, or for yourself?

He pushed that to the side. It made no difference debating this with himself. She was here, she was his wife. And he would conduct their marriage, and raise his child in the way that he saw fit, and it was not for her to tell him otherwise.

'You mean well, Beatrice,' he said. 'I know you do. You are a kind, sweet girl...'

'You make it sound as though you are speaking of a kitten. Kind and sweet and well meaning. But you forget, Your Grace, that kittens have claws, and you have vastly underestimated mine.'

She turned to begin storming away from him, and he caught her by the arm.

The action shocked her, clearly it did; her eyes went wide, her cheeks pink. That was what he noticed first. Then after that, he noticed the way that her skin felt beneath his touch. Soft. Warm. And he was transported back to that garden. To that moment when he had realised just what a lovely woman she had become. And perhaps that was why it was so easy to dismiss her now. To turn all of this into a treatise on her inexperience. To write her off as a child, because as long as he could think of her as such, he had an easier time keeping his hands off her.

'You may have claws, kitten,' he said, his voice soft and stern. 'But do not forget that I could pick you up with one hand if I so chose. I do not deny that you possess a certain amount of ferocity, but I have an iron hand, and you would do well to remember that.'

'Threats?'

'Not deadly threats,' he said, pushing hard at the bonds of propriety that he had laid out for himself. 'But perhaps you do require a punishment. For all that he has kept you hemmed in your entire life, Hugh is quite indulgent towards you.'

Her lips parted, her breasts quickening. 'You do not know of what you speak.'

'Perhaps not. But I know more about you than you might think.'

'If you knew anything about me, you would not treat me as you do. You would not ignore me for days on end. I am little more than an antiquity to you, set up on a shelf in this house and left to gather dust.'

She jerked away from him. 'You do not have the authority to punish an object.'

'I have the authority to do whatever I wish.'

'Perhaps. But where is the glory to be had in unchecked authority? Authority that must be taken.'

And her words tugged at his gut, because she had hit right against the very thing he knew deeply to be true. There was no joy in wielding authority when the supplicant was not willing. But this was not a game to be played in a bedroom. This was…

What was it? He didn't seem to know.

Neither did she. That much was clear. Her eyes burned bright, with both rage and excitement. And he knew, he absolutely knew that she had no idea why this battle excited her. He knew all too well that it fired his blood. And he felt nothing but contempt for himself. Over his lack of control. Because he had attempted it at this moment. Brought it to this place. Not because it was an accident, because he was actually threatening to punish her, but because he wanted to tease the fire inside her. Because he wanted to push that limit and see how far it might go. She was not a simpering miss. He didn't mind a simpering miss, particularly when she was playing a role. But he found he responded to the wilfulness in her. She liked to fight, did Beatrice. And that said more about her than she knew.

But she moved away from him, effectively placing herself in a safer spot. Smart girl. It was better that way. Better that she end this now.

'You're right,' she said. 'This is the first time I have seen you in your real life. And I thought that I knew you based on what I saw when you were in the presence of my brother. But I do not know you. I will not make commentary on you. However, I feel strongly about William.'

'Why is that?'

'Because I see myself in him. And you might find that silly, or you may not believe it, but I do. But it is true. Protection at what cost, Briggs?'

'He does not…'

'As you said, he does not always show it. I understand that everyone around me, everyone in my life, was simply trying to make things better for me. Perhaps not my father, but my mother and Hugh wanted only that I should be safe. But they wanted my safety so very much that they did not consider risk is part of living. But it must be. Because there is so much that I have not tasted, so much that I feel I have not done. Survival, *breathing*, cannot be the end of it. I am certain of that fact.'

'But without at least that there is nothing,' he said.

'William isn't going to die of a trip to London. He just might find it difficult.'

'I only meant if we were speaking of you, Beatrice.'

'Thank you for thinking of me,' she said. 'But I'm tired of it. I wish to think of more.'

And as he watched her leave, he could not escape the sensation that he was failing yet again. That he was not… It was not any better off with Beatrice than he had been with Serena. And worse, he wondered if Beatrice would be any happier.

Chapter Eight

Beatrice wondered if she would ever have a peaceful night's sleep. She worried about William and listened for his cries while she should be sleeping.

She rarely saw Briggs.

And as each lonely day stretched on—with Alice the governess not warming to her, with most meals eaten alone and nights stretching on endlessly, she realised this was truly no different than Bybee House.

Except she did not have her mother. She had no one here who cared about her at all.

Except perhaps William, but it was very difficult to say. Some days with him were lovely. Others…

He often became angry and lashed out. Afternoons seemed very hard for him. Beatrice could understand why Briggs wanted to protect him, but he was so bright and brilliant, and seeing him sequestered in isolation—as she was—felt wrong.

When she had lived at Bybee House she had co-cooned herself in her innocence. She had not wished to look too deeply at the world around her.

Choosing to look at the bright colours of the frescoes and not too closely at the chips and cracks in the paint.

Not searching herself deeply for the truths of her parents' lives or their actions. She had instead focused on her own world. The one she created in the gardens alone. In her secret friendships.

In fantasy.

Yet her decision to fling herself into James's arms had been the first step away from that and into reality.

She had landed somewhere much…harder with Briggs.

In all the ways that could be taken.

Her foray into the real world was difficult and she felt as if she was shedding layers of down, her insulation against the harsher truths of life falling away.

She was not sure if she liked it.

But she could not help William if she turned away.

She was trying to sort out exactly how to broach the topic with Briggs, over a buttered roll with preserves, when Gates the butler walked into the room.

'Your Grace, Sir James Prescott to see you. Shall I tell him you're at home?'

Her heart lifted.

James.

The idea of seeing her friend made her almost giddy.

If Gates thought less of her because a man had come to call on her he did not show it. She had a feeling that had more to do with his sense of propriety regarding his position than it did with whether or not he actually judged her.

When James entered the room, it was as if the sun shone twice as bright on the pale blue and gold. And he was golden. Like the sun. She'd forgotten what it was like to have someone smile at her.

Gates nodded and left the room, leaving the doors open wide.

'James,' she said, 'I am so, so pleased you've called. Sit and I'll ring for tea.'

'Thank you, Bea,' he said, sitting and looking at her, his expression intent, and there was something about having her friend there, having someone who truly knew her and understood her look at her, when Briggs had been ignoring her, that made her eyes fill with tears. James's expression became alarmed. 'Are you well? He isn't being an ogre?'

She blinked heavily, annoyed at herself. 'He being my *husband*?' She dashed at one rogue tear that had slid down her cheek.

'Yes.'

'Why would he be an ogre?'

'You seem distressed.'

'Yes, but why would it make you think he is...unkind to me?'

James hesitated. 'There is a lot of talk about the Duke of Brigham. And his...proclivities. Though, I should not pay heed to gossip of that nature for clear reasons.'

Beatrice blinked, feeling as if she were missing a piece of the conversation again.

'To be as delicate as possible, he is a man of exotic tastes. Some might say perverse, though I never would.'

Briggs? Perverse?

She did not have a clear idea of what that might mean, except it called to mind someone who was twisted and warped in some way. One thing she could not imagine was her brother being friends with someone that were true of.

Much less allow her to marry him.

You are a ward, not a wife...

'I've seen no proof of anything of the kind,' she said, trying to smile.

'Probably a good thing.'

'What is that supposed to mean?'

James sighed and sat in the chair opposite her. 'That you are sweet. And men like him are not.'

'People keep saying I am sweet. Why is that? What have I done to suggest that I am?'

'You...'

'I am stupid, is what I am. I do not know enough people, I have not been educated broadly on enough topics, I have not done enough.'

'You are not stupid,' James said. 'You are innocent.'

'Well, I am tired of it.'

'Do you wish for him to take your innocence?'

She suddenly felt that same warmth she'd felt in the carriage. She was embarrassed, but...but James had told her his secrets. Secrets that could see him jailed. What did she have to fear with her friend? This dear, lovely friend who had put his faith in her in such a real way. 'I... It would be better if I knew what that meant.'

'There is nothing to know. Beatrice, I knew what I was, what I wanted, before I knew details or specifics. You do not need to know the full list of things one might do, to know you wish them.' She still felt confused, but she couldn't be angry because his smile was so gentle. 'The question is, do you want to be closer to him?'

'I...'

'Do you want to kiss him?'

Her face went hot. 'I do... I...'

'Then kiss him, Beatrice.'

'He said...'

'That has nothing to do with what he *wants*.'

Bea's breathing became short, harsh, and she could feel her heart beating in her temples. 'James, I cannot...'

'Whatever he says, Beatrice, you are his wife.'

She let out a long breath. 'Enough about me. Please. What are you doing?'

'I came to tell you I'm leaving.'

'Leaving?'

'Yes, I...am travelling to Rome with a friend.' The way he said friend was heavy.

'Will you stay there?'

'For a while at least.' He smiled. 'I'm happy, Beatrice.'

'I am very glad for you, I...'

She felt him before she saw him and when she looked up, her husband was in the doorway with all the subtlety of a storm. 'Your Grace,' James said, standing quickly. 'I came to say goodbye to your wife. I'm leaving the country.'

Briggs's eyes flickered over him. 'You must be James.'

He did not sound friendly, or impressed.

'Yes,' he said.

'In the future if you wish to call on my wife, you will ensure I am present.'

'He's my friend,' Beatrice said.

'He is the man you intended to marry. And I'll not be made a cuckold in my own home.'

'If you cannot give any credit to my honour, at least give it to hers,' James said.

Briggs looked at him, hard. 'I have nothing to fear from you, do I?'

The side of James's mouth kicked up. 'No. I am leaving, though, so if you wish to have me arrested it will have to be quick.'

'I am the last person on earth to have a man arrested for his inclinations.'

'Ah. I did wonder.' James turned to her. 'Remember what we talked about. Be you, Beatrice. And if that's not sweet, then don't be sweet.' He leaned in and kissed her cheek, and the feeling of affection that overwhelmed her nearly brought her to tears.

So few and far between were connections in her life.

'I will see you again, when I return.'

'Yes,' she said. 'Come to dinner. Bring your friend.'

He left her there with a squeeze of her hand and when she turned to face Briggs, his eyes were like ice.

'What were you thinking?'

Briggs couldn't account for the rage that was currently pouring through his veins.

'I was thinking that I would take tea with my friend, who came to sit with me. Which is more than you have done, Your Grace.'

He knew this side of her. He had seen it when she'd pushed at Hugh in her bedchamber. He had often admired her spirit, but he admired it much less now that she chose to use it against him.

'If my household were not so loyal to me, the scandal you might have caused…'

She laughed. 'Here I thought married women entertaining other men was de rigueur.'

The rage in his blood threatened to boil over. 'Not in my house.'

His tone was hard, uncompromising, and he could see the way she responded to it. The way her cheeks lit up like a beacon on a hill, a signal to a man like him that she would melt like butter if he were to place his hand on the back of her neck now…

She would go to her knees willingly.

He shut that thought down with ruthless precision.

'We are leaving for London in the morning,' he said, ready for a change of subject.

He had been enraged seeing her in here with another man, regardless of the fact he was not a man who would be interested in her. Regardless of the fact he was not supposed to want her.

He was eager to get out of this house.

He had grown to see Maynard Park as his own. For some reason, though, the demons of his childhood felt close now. Perhaps because it was the very beginning of summer, with flowers beginning to bloom.

A reminder.

His father had died this time of year.

His father had also destroyed everything Briggs had cared about in June, and humiliated him while he did it.

'Briggs, I do wish you'd reconsider about William.'

The mention of William on the heels of the thoughts about his father brought him up short.

'No,' he said, his voice sharper than intended.

'Didn't your parents…?'

'I went nowhere. I stayed here.'

'Were you happy with that?'

Sometimes. Because it had meant living as he chose. Only doing what he enjoyed. Losing himself in his own world.

'You want to make everything simple,' he said, his voice rough. 'It is not simple. You are angry that you've been protected all your life, but you can't know whether or not that protection was necessary. You cannot know if you would have died without the intervention you were given.'

'I...no. I don't suppose I can know that.'

'You resent it but it might be the very thing that saved you. William may be lonely, but being exposed to other children might not be the best thing for him. It would not have been for me. I...am angry at my father. But on that he might have been right.' It cost him to say it, and to the end of his life he would not know why he had.

Except Beatrice was honest.

In all things.

And there was something about that honesty that seemed to demand it in return.

If there was one thing a man such as himself valued, it was the necessary balances in life.

She looked at him, her gaze far too insightful. 'Why are you angry at your father?'

'It is not important,' he said, his jaw going tense.

'It must be. For you to be angry after all this time.'

She was so guileless in her questions. As if she merely wished to know.

And it compelled him to answer.

'My father was cruel. He enjoyed that. Enjoyed making others feel small. He wielded power and control over those weaker than himself. And do you know what that makes him?'

'What?' she asked, her voice shrunken to a whisper.

'A coward. A real man, a man of honour, does not use his power in that way.'

'You don't use your power that way,' she said.

He looked at her and he wanted to...he wanted to

cup her chin and hold her steady, hold her gaze until she had to look away.

He could use his power, his strength, to make her feel good.

And just then he felt desperate to do that. It would ease the ache in him as well, this restless fury that had been building since he had brought her here.

Perhaps it is her.

Another reminder of all you once hoped for.

All you can never have.

He pushed that aside.

He could not have her. Not like that. And he would not allow lingering memories of Serena, or of his father, to push him to violate his friendship with Hugh.

To put Beatrice at risk.

'No,' he said, finally. 'I do not.'

'What did your father…?'

'My father liked to humiliate. He liked those around him to feel small. Undone. And he could do so with a few well-placed words.' And actions. His father had not hesitated to take away whatever Briggs had found himself obsessed with.

He would wait, though.

Until he had invested time and himself into it. Would wait until the loss of it had an exacting, heavy cost.

'Briggs, I…'

'I am not an object to be pitied. My father is rotting in the ground and I am the Duke of Brigham.' He smiled, and he knew it did not reach his eyes. 'I may not be perfect in regard to William but what I want is for him to avoid shame.'

'I believe you. I do know that you only have his best interests at heart. I…'

'You just don't trust me. Because you're a foolish girl who has seen nothing of the world and yet is convinced she knows the right way of it.'

He successfully cowed her then. But she rallied, and quickly. 'Perhaps that is true. But my innocence has been forced upon me. I can learn. But what I see in William is not the product of inexperience. Quite the opposite. I recognise myself and it pains me.'

'You see loneliness. Because it is what you felt. I did not feel lonely here.'

'What did you feel?'

He felt a slow smile spread over his face. 'Rage.'

Chapter Nine

Beatrice knew that she should be excited. They were headed to London just before the Season started, and Briggs had promised her new dresses.

She was not feeling excited.

Not after the way everything had happened between the two of them. She was still upset about William, and Briggs's refusal to bring him. She was still upset about what had happened with James the day before, and still...

Deeply confused by the conversation they'd had after.

She was a jumble of feelings. None of which were sweet or strictly innocent.

Kiss him.

Her heart jolted. She did not wish to kiss him. She was angry at him.

For his heavy-handed behaviour. For the way he made her feel.

For what he made her want.

She was still ruminating on that, standing at the entry of the home, when William, Alice, and several more bags came down the stairs. 'What is this?' she asked Briggs, as he appeared alongside her.

'I thought about what you said,' he returned, his voice clipped.

'You thought about what I said?'

'Yes,' he said.

'And you changed your mind.'

'Yes,' he said. 'I changed my mind. William shall accompany us to London for the Season.'

It was difficult to tell if the boy was pleased or not. But she very much hoped that he was. She hoped that he would enjoy his trip, and she even hoped that she could be the one to take him to some of those places he was so interested in. Places she had never been either.

It was a five-hour carriage ride to London, and William was alternatively fidgety, fussy, quiet, and extremely talkative. He spent a good hour of the trip telling Beatrice each and every fact he possessed about Italian architecture. And there were quite a lot of them. Later she realised that it was the same time in the afternoon that she had first arrived at Maynard Park. When William had been screaming inconsolably.

They had to stop so that the little boy could relieve himself, and they paused the carriage, and rather than his governess accompanying him, it was Briggs who got out of the carriage.

Alice made a study out of avoiding any sort of eye contact with Beatrice. Which she supposed was probably common enough, but she didn't have anyone to talk to. She was older than governesses often were. She reminded Bea nothing of the little frothy blonde creatures her father had favoured putting her in the care of.

Though she had a feeling her governesses had not been selected because of the care they might give *her*. A thought that made her skin feel coated in oil.

She squirmed in her seat and thought about getting out simply to stretch her legs and get some distance between herself and the unfriendly woman.

But a moment later she heard a great wail, and the governess immediately departed the carriage. Beatrice wasn't far behind. William was on the ground, refusing to be moved. Briggs looked...grim, stone-faced, but determined.

'William,' he said, not raising his voice at all. 'We must get back in the carriage now.'

'I'm tired.' William was flopped, utterly, limply across the ground.

'It doesn't matter if you're tired. You cannot sleep here. You may sleep in the carriage.'

'I can't sleep in the carriage. It's too noisy.'

'William.'

'I can't. I can't. I can't.'

And that began a period of long repetition. Denials and recriminations. The young boy thrashed on the ground like a fish, and refused to be settled. He ground his heels into the soft mud, kicking and flinging rocks into the air.

Beatrice was frozen. She had no idea what to do, what to say. She felt useless.

And for the first time she wished she were back at Bybee House. Where she was safe. Where she could not cause the harm that she had clearly caused here by begging Briggs to bring William.

Finally, Briggs plucked him up from the ground and

held him as close to his chest as possible while the boy squirmed.

'Back in the carriage,' he bit out to both Beatrice and the governess.

The governess obeyed quickly, but Beatrice stood and stared at him.

'Do you find there is something to gawk at?' he said.

'No,' Beatrice said. 'I'm not gawking.'

'You do rather a good imitation of someone who is.'

He moved past her, opening the carriage door and depositing William inside. William continued to howl unhappily.

'Get inside,' he said.

And she obeyed.

'William,' she said, trying to keep her tone placating. 'Didn't you want to see things in London?'

But he was simply screaming now, and there was nothing, seemingly nothing at all that could reach him. She did not know what to do, or how to proceed. And Briggs was only sitting there grim-faced, staring straight ahead.

'William,' she tried again, moving forward.

And was met with a short slap on the hand, directly from William, who screamed again, 'I can't.'

It didn't hurt, his slap, but it shocked her, and she drew back, clutching her hand.

Briggs leaned forward, plucked William up and held him in his arms, his hold firm, but not harming him in any way. 'William,' he said. 'You may not hit. Ever.'

'I can't. *I can't.*'

'William,' Briggs said.

'I'm not William.'

And neither of them said anything after that. They simply let him scream. Until he tired himself out, with only thirty minutes to spare before they arrived in London. The town house was lovely. But she could barely take it in. Or the excitement of being in London. She was too enervated by everything that had occurred on the ride. By how badly she had miscalculated. No wonder Briggs was so protective of William. No wonder he had been concerned about taking this journey. It was not because he hadn't wanted to take it on board. It was because it was devastating to watch William unravel in that fashion. And she hadn't realised it. Of course she hadn't. She had not listened.

Not really.

She had been so certain that she knew best, and she had been wrong.

William had drifted to sleep by the time they got inside, and it was Briggs who carried the limp little boy up the stairs. He said nothing to Beatrice, and she could hardly blame him.

'Your Grace.' The housekeeper in London, Mrs Dinsdale, put her hand on Beatrice's shoulder, as if sensing her distress.

'Oh, yes,' she said.

'You will find a lady's maid waiting for you. You may go and get freshened up for dinner.'

She dreaded it. Dreaded sharing a meal with Briggs. Of course he never shared meals with her out at Maynard Park. So perhaps, he would not do so here.

She was escorted to her room and introduced to the maid, and a collection of dresses she had never seen before. She was wrapped in something lovely and soft, a beautiful mint-green gown that scooped low, with no fichu to provide coverage for her bosom.

Her hair was arranged in a complicated fashion, with a string of pearls draped around her head like a crown.

How lovely she looked to take dinner by herself.

She went downstairs, her heart thundering madly, and predictably found the dining room... Empty.

'Might I take dinner in my bedchamber?' she asked one of the attending servants.

'Of course, Your Grace,' the man said.

She went back upstairs, and there she sat, looking quite the prettiest she ever had, in solitude.

Dinner was beautiful. And far too extensive for only her, but she ate her way through each course all the same. Mackerel with fennel and mint, roasted game, and pickled vegetables. Followed by a lovely tray of colourful marzipan, which she found she overindulged in.

She did not stop eating until her stomach turned.

And then she had her maid undress her, take her hair down, and put the pearls back in their box. And she looked in the mirror and found that she had become Beatrice again. Just her usual self, with nothing of any great interest about her at all. And she felt exceedingly sorry for herself.

You should feel sorry for William.

She did not understand. But then, he was a child. It was likely he did not have the ability to connect the fact that the journey was what was going to take him to those places that he longed so to see. If he could not endure a journey such as this, how did he ever hope to reach Italy? But these were all things a seven-year-old could likely not reason, she told herself. But it did not make her less frustrated.

Nor did it help her sleep. Long after she should have extinguished her candle, she tried to read.

She tried to read *Emma*, but found she was too furious at the contents to enjoy it. And the illustrated compendium of birds was not compelling enough to hold her interest.

She paced the length of the room, practically wearing a hole in the floor. She looked out of the window, and felt compelled to escape. As she had done so many times at Bybee House.

If she could've crawled out of her own skin she would have done so, but failing that, she simply contented herself with fleeing the house.

And so, she did so here.

She opened the door to the bedchamber and quietly made her way down the stairs.

She did not know if there was a back garden, but she assumed so. And she was not disappointed. It was a lovely space, bathed in moonlight, with a massive fountain, surrounded by several statues.

Nude statues.

It was *very* Roman. William, she thought with grim humour, would likely find it quite interesting.

She found herself staring at a naked warrior, clothed only in a helmet, which she felt left him vulnerable in many other ways.

Briggs had asked her if she knew what made a man and a woman different.

Of course she knew. She was not an idiot.

He had said it was so they could… Fit together. Make a child. The idea made her flush all over. For imagining such an intimate part of herself fitted against…

Kiss him.

She swallowed hard.

Who gets to decide?

She circled the statue, examining the powerful

thighs, the rather muscular-looking derrière. At least, this took her mind off the disastrous carriage ride. Yes. It was a very different sort of body. Though it was made of stone. Perhaps that was why it appeared so hard. She knew Briggs was solid though. Not like her at all.

A sound made her turn, and she saw Briggs, standing in the doorway. He was not dressed for bed, rather, he was dressed to go out. He was standing there, looking through the glass. And she felt inexplicably quite caught out.

She moved away from the statue, and waited to see what he might do. If he would turn away and continue on as he had intended to do, or if he would come out to her.

She did not have to wait long for her answer.

The door opened.

'And are you trying to tempt brigands to scale my garden wall and kidnap you?' he asked. The words were like the Briggs she'd known for much of her life. The tone was not.

'I had no aspirations of such,' she said, turning away from him.

'You only wished to leer at my statuary?'

'I was not leering. I was admiring the artistry.'

'Of course,' he said. 'How could I be so foolish? A lady such as yourself would never do anything half so…interesting.'

'Briggs…'

'I only came to check that you were well.'

'I am not well,' she said. 'I fear that I made things incredibly difficult by pushing you to bring William on the trip, and I… I am deeply… Deeply sorry, and so very… I did not mean to upset him. Or you.'

'But the end result is that you have,' Briggs said. 'And there is nothing to be done for that.'

'I am sorry,' she said.

'It doesn't matter,' he said.

'It clearly does.'

'No. It does not. I made the decision in the end to bring him. It is done.' He looked past her, into the darkness, then back at her. 'Do not stray from the garden.'

'I would not.'

'You are in London, now, and you must take care. You will not leave the house without accompaniment. This garden being the exception.'

'Yes. Sorry, I had quite forgotten that I was your ward, and in no way your equal.'

'Even if you were my wife, you would not be my equal.'

She sucked in a sharp breath at the barb, that she had a feeling did not reflect what he thought about anything, but rather was designed to harm her. And it had. Why was she so fragile where he was concerned? It made no sense. And yet, he made her feel as if she was made of broken glass.

Why did he have this power over her?

It was something beyond friendship, for theirs was no easy companionship. She resented the way he avoided her when she should not care about it at all. His disdain hurt. She did not understand how they had got here.

It had changed since he had touched her by the fire in her brother's study.

And again after he'd pushed her on the swing.

And most of all after they had married, after the carriage ride.

It should have worked, this arrangement. And yet nothing about it did.

'Of course not.'

He turned away from her.

'And where is it you are going?' she asked.

'I do not have to answer to you.'

'That in and of itself is an answer. And *such* an answer,' she said. 'Why you do not simply wish to tell me...'

'I am going to a brothel, Beatrice, are you familiar with the term?'

His face looked cruel now, and she hated this. This was not the man who had brought her sweets. This was a dark and furious stranger, the man who had compelled her to stare across the ballroom on that night, the man who captured her breath.

She knew that he was angry, but there was something in his cold, quiet fury that made her feel sick.

'No,' she said. 'I... I don't know what that means.'

Perhaps it pertained to his duties at the House of Lords. But judging by the expression on his face she knew that it did not.

For that would not hurt her. And right now, he wished to hurt her. She could feel it.

'It is where a man goes when he wishes to purchase the company of a woman.'

That immediately brought to mind an image of Briggs sitting down to tea with a lady, and she was absolutely certain that was the wrong image to be in the middle of her head, and yet there it was.

'Still confused?' he asked, and his tone was unkind.

'Stop it,' she said, feeling angry now. 'You are aware of the gap in my knowledge on certain things, given the cloistered life that I had led, and it is one thing to acknowledge them, but it is quite another to cruelly take pleasure in them.'

'I cannot help what I cruelly take pleasure in, Beatrice. Perhaps I am a much crueller man than you have any idea of.'

'I should hope not. For I am your ward. And what ward should like a cruel guardian?'

His lips curved. Beautiful. Painful. 'I suspect you might enjoy my cruelty.'

'I am *not currently*,' she bit out. 'As it happens.'

'When I speak of female company, I mean shagging, Beatrice.'

She wanted to howl at him in frustration. 'I don't know what shagging is.'

'It is what men and women do. And it is not for procreation. It is for pleasure. A man and his wife might engage in such acts for procreation, but there are a great many things that a person can do to pursue pleasure.'

Her head was pounding, her temples aching.

'And you are… You are off to seek them with other women.'

'I will not seek them with you.'

'And so you go to a brothel to seek them out with other women. And you would throw it in my face while not giving me information on exactly what it entails. So if you wish to harm me, do so by speaking plainly, rather than speaking around the truth of the matter.'

'I am off to screw my way to oblivion. To forget everything that happened this day. To forget that you are my wife. To forget that my son is here. That is what I intend to do. And if you should like a more graphic description of all that I shall do, I am sorry to disappoint you. I can see that you are quite interested in a man's cock, judging by how closely you were studying the statue. Mine will be inside another woman tonight.'

It was so cool it took her breath away, and she still could not quite sort out why, except the idea of him sharing intimacies she was barely able to wrap her mind around made her want to vomit in the nearest shrub. And she knew that he wanted her to be hurt. That was the clearest and most obvious piece. What he was saying was designed to be harmful.

And he well knew it.

And before she could gather a response, he turned and walked away. She stood there, stunned for a moment, breathing in the sharp night air. And then she ran after him. Just in time to watch him walk out through the front door.

She stood there, feeling tender, hurt. She did not want him to touch another woman. She was beginning to piece it all together, of course. For these were all the mysterious acts that must follow kissing. She had never even partaken in such a thing, and...

Of course he would seek out other company. Even if she were his wife in truth he would likely find her boring, and her ignorance tiring.

She was tired of her ignorance.

She was tired. Tired of everyone else deciding what was best for her. Tired of her own limitations.

She was tired.

And still, she could not sleep.

She decided that she would wait up for him to arrive home. Even if it destroyed her to do it.

Usually, a visit to Madame Lissanne's was like a visit to an old friend. The velvet brocade and access typically felt like a homecoming. But not tonight. Tonight, his stomach was acid. He was angry, and he had taken it out quite unfairly on Beatrice. Beyond that, he had been intentionally as crass and mean as possible, and it was not what he had promised Hugh that he would do as husband to his sister. Truly, the only piece of his word that he had kept was that he had not visited his desires upon her. No. He would do that here. If Pamela was available, he would see her. She was curvy and lush, and excelled in her submission. Her demure manner would be a welcome change to Beatrice's sulky mouth.

Here, he was treated like a king. Here, he was given a glass of his preferred whisky, and ushered to a bedchamber to wait for a woman who suited his desires and was available. And indeed, it was Pamela. She offered him a shy smile, her eyes not meeting his.

And he waited. For a rising feeling of excitement. For desire. For something. He waited to feel what he should for a woman this beautiful. A woman he knew performed exceedingly well.

She made her way across the room, to where he sat, then dropped to her knees before him. She reached forward, making for the buttons on his trousers.

'No,' he said. 'I did not tell you to touch me.'

Colour swept across her cheeks, and she looked away. 'I'm sorry, Your Grace.'

And for some reason, when she said those words, he thought only of Beatrice. And how the words sounded on her lips. And he felt… Guilt. Guilt that he was here when he had married Beatrice. Most of all, over the way that he had treated her prior to coming to the brothel.

'Stand. Take your dress off.'

She complied, removing her gown, and revealing that she had nothing on underneath.

Her body was lovely, her mons waxed clean, and normally, he would be feeling some sense of desire or excitement. He felt nothing. And perversely, she looked absolutely aroused by his complete uninterest. If only his uninterest were feigned. But it was not.

He could obviously proceed. But he was too furious. And the woman he needed to be dealing with was not here.

'I'm sorry.' He stood, walked forward and grabbed hold of her chin. 'I'm not in need of your services tonight. I will still issue payment.'

'Have I done something wrong?' Whether or not hers was a desire to truly please, or concern she was losing a valuable client, he did not know. But it didn't matter either.

That she made it impossible to tell was why she was so good at what she did.

'The problem is with me. And I must go and sort it out.' The money would be put on his ledger, and he would settle the account later. There was no need for anything quite so common as for money to change hands then and there. He walked out of the den of iniquity and on to the far too busy streets. Then he began the journey home. And he called himself every foul name he could think of.

He tore through the front door of the town house, intent on taking himself up to his bedchamber. And he saw that she was still outside.

He could see that sweet, white nightgown, which she had been wearing the night that he had come upon her in the swing.

She turned, eyes wide. 'Seems a rather short visit to a brothel,' she said, but her face betrayed her shock.

'You have no idea how long such matters should take.'

'Perhaps not. But given the severity of your manner when you left, I expected it to be a rather long night.'

'And here you are.'

'Do not flatter yourself. If you are suggesting that you think I was waiting for you...'

'I would never suggest such a thing,' he said.

'Why are you here?'

'Because,' he said, taking a step towards her, 'of you.'

'What have I done?'

His blood was boiling now. And he knew that he should not move even one fraction of an inch towards her. But he did. He did, and as he did, his desire drew up tight inside him like a bow. And he was on the edge of control. Which did not happen to him. He was a man who prized control above all else. It was his linchpin. The most important thing to a man such as him. He could never afford to be out of control. Not ever.

'Ask me your questions.'

'I have no more questions for you. Except perhaps why you insist on treating me so poorly?'

'You wish to know the secrets of the universe. You wish to insert yourself into my life. Do you wish for me to stop protecting you?'

He could see her running quick mental calculations. He could also see that she had no idea what he was asking. And it was not a kindness that he was doing it.

'You wish to step into this role in William's life. You wish to understand the world. You wish to be trusted to go to war. Then you tell me now. What is it you wish to learn?'

'Everything,' she said, the words exiting her mouth in a rush.

And then he reached the end of it. The end of everything.

And he took a step forward, wrapping his arm around her waist and drawing her up to his chest. He could feel her breasts pressed against him, lush and supple. And the way she looked up at him, her eyes full of wonder, did something to him that he could not adequately describe.

He could kiss her. But instead, he gave in to a much darker temptation. He put his hand on the back of her head, grabbed hold of the thick braid that hung down the centre of her back, and tugged, hard.

Chapter Ten

Beatrice's heart was thundering like a galloping horse. The sharp pain that started at the base of her neck spread out over her skull, delightful prickles of sensation cascading over her, and uncomfortable warmth.

And she felt... Fortified. Strong. Held tight there in Briggs's hold. And she could not understand why this was happening. Why he was now standing so close to her, why he was making her feel this way. And why he had the power to do so.

He had told her that for some pleasure and pain was one in the same. And the deep, curling sensation at her midsection made her feel he had been right. And more unsettling, she had a feeling he had known he would be right about her.

He was looking at her with a blazing heat that spoke only of confidence. He had known that he could do this. That she would not cry out or pull away from him. He had known that she would want to press herself more closely to him.

It was his certainty that rooted her to the spot.

It was his certainty that intrigued her.

That infuriated her.

The certainty of this... This man who was infinitely harder than the stone statues all around them.

He pulled again, and forced her chin to tilt upwards. Tears gathered at the corners of her eyes, and she withstood. She felt proud. Infinitely so. For she was strong. And free.

Here, in this moment, she felt as if she was proving it. Not just to him, but to herself. To anyone who had ever found her weak.

This was her moment, to step into the role of warrior. Prove she could withstand.

And that thought alone brought her an infinite sense of satisfaction.

And then his mouth, oh, his mouth. It was on hers, and it was not the stuff of romance and softness. It was a hard sort of heat that she had never imagined. It was devastation. Each movement of his lips was expert and, combined with the intense tug on her hair, made her feel as if she were drowning.

Oh, she felt she was drowning.

And then, he slid his tongue between the seam of her lips, and her legs folded. But he caught her. By her hair. And the resulting tug drew a scream from her lips that he swallowed. His hold was firm, and he did not let her collapse completely. Briggs would never let her collapse completely, and in spite of everything, she felt that to be true. In spite of all the anger that had just passed between them, she trusted that.

She trusted him.

She found herself being pushed backwards, right up against that naked male statue. Because she had been right. Briggs was just as hard. But he was hot.

The marble was cold beneath her back, and it dawned on her slowly, as she shifted her gaze for a moment to stare at the statue, that the very hard thing she could feel pressed against her stomach was…

Well, if she was correct, the statue paled in comparison to Briggs.

He was kissing her. She could not quite believe it. Did that mean that he… Did that mean that he wanted her?

She was so new to this. To the idea of desire. Of want. But he had said that people did this for reasons other than procreation. He had said that it was about pleasure. And pain.

And then she found the top of her gown, the chemise beneath, being pushed away, revealing her breasts.

He took a step away, only for a moment, and stared down at her, his expression hungry.

She was confident in that. His expression held hunger. She did not know how, but it was as if some ancient wisdom inside her body had materialised for this moment.

And she did not feel confused. Somehow, the absurdity of her lips meeting his, of his tongue sliding against hers, crystallised these mysteries, and if anyone had asked her how it would do that, she would have said she did not know. She would've said it was impossible. She would have said that she did not wish to be licked by Briggs, and yet now she knew she did. And that she wished to lick him in return.

He moved forward, holding her breast with one large hand. And then he pinched her. Slowly, carefully, applying even pressure to one tightened bud. And then, he made it hard.

She cried out, pain radiating through her body, an answering echo between her thighs. And it was like an exultant hallelujah chorus. A burst of bright, sharp hope echoing through her body.

A wash of strength pouring itself over her like liquid gold, coating all that she was and reinforcing her.

She felt like a warrior in this moment.

Real. True.

She felt weightless. And she felt fearless. And then, he moved to the other side, but he did not build his pressure quite so slowly; this time he clamped down, his eyes making contact with hers as he did so.

Until she had to let her head fall back against the statue's abdomen and surrender. She closed her eyes and shivered, shook, as pleasure and pain mingled together until she could not sort one from the other. Indeed, she wondered if they were different.

For one showed her that she could withstand, and the other was the reward for that patience. For that endurance. Then he fastened his mouth to her neck, sucking hard, before returning to her lips and kissing her, kissing her until she couldn't breathe. Until she was senseless. But then, perhaps she had already been senseless. Then he bit her lip at the same time he pinched her again, and she felt something unravel inside her, and then bloom. And it radiated through her in a wave. On and on and she could barely breathe. Could barely think. And it reminded her of dying. Like when she would lose her breath and float towards that space where there was no sound, no light.

And then bursts of fireworks.

The vision of something bigger, greater than herself.

And when it subsided, she shuddered. And slid down the statue. All the way to the ground.

And Briggs stood above her, his gaze something like triumphant, and something like terrifying.

He bent down, and gripped her chin. 'You did well.'

And she realised she was shaking. Shivering from the cold and from something else that she could not name. She found herself gathered up into his arms and held close to his chest. And then he lifted her up off the ground, and carried her into the house, carried her up the stairs. Her heart leapt like a wild thing. She didn't know where he was taking her. Or what would happen next. He took her to her room. And laid her gently on the bed, his manner suddenly soothing and entirely different to the way it had been moments before.

'Sleep,' he said.

'Briggs,' she whispered.

'Please,' he said. 'Do not speak.'

'But I need to… I need to know. Are you going back to the brothel?'

'No,' he said, his tone hard.

'Please don't.'

'I do not answer to you, darling wife.'

'I know. I do not wish you to go, though. And I would hope that that matters, whether or not you must obey me.'

'I will not return to the brothel tonight.'

And that she knew was the best she would get from him. But was that what he went to the brothel to do? To touch other women like that? To make them… She had no idea what he had done to her. She had never felt anything like it. It was like nothing she had ever experienced before, and she was desperate to experience it again. But also terrified. Because the way that it made her feel... Desperate and aching and restless inside... Well, she did not particularly care for that. That, she found, was almost entirely unbearable. She wanted him to hold her. She realised that with stunning clarity. But all of the confidence that she felt in that moment, all of the strength and brilliance and perfection seemed to fall away from her. She was simply... Undone. And she hated it. As much as she had loved all that had come before.

For a moment, she had felt strong. For a moment, she felt like a warrior. For a moment, she had felt like a woman. And now she was just back to being Beatrice. And it was enough to make her dissolve.

Chapter Eleven

Briggs was in hell. Because he had spectacularly ruined everything last night. And she had been... She had been a triumph. She was everything that he had suspected she was. And what a cruel joke that his best friend's younger sister should be made quite so perfectly in such a twisted, glorious fashion that she could fit up against every kink in him? It was a cruelty. But she had come apart in his arms from just a bit of pain and pleasure, and he had a feeling that were he to push her further, faster, they would find heights together that... It did not bear thinking about.

Today, he had to deal with his son.

Today, he would be taking him to see the sights around London. For they had endured the trip all for that. On one score he suspected Beatrice might be right. That if William had the distraction of those things which he was most interested in, he would weather everything else quite well.

And after that nightmare of the trip, there had to be some compensation. He was practised enough in the art of indulging himself in a bit of mastery and then going back to being the Duke of Brigham, and father to William, without allowing any of the night's previous indulgence to affect him in any way. Or to linger into the day. And yet he felt affected by this. By his indiscretion in the garden with Beatrice.

An indiscretion with your wife? A new low, and who knew you could still reach those?

He would laugh, but it wasn't funny. Nothing about the damned situation was funny.

He decided to find William and try to ply the boy with toast and drinking chocolate prior to presenting him with the day's itinerary. If he knew one thing about managing William, it was that an itinerary was very important, but he had to be sure to stick to it, because if he did not, then his son would be sure to let him know all the ways in which he had failed. And the point of this was not to fail.

But when he arrived at his son's room, Beatrice was already there, sitting on the floor beside him, engaged in what looked like a very intense conversation about shoes.

'Good morning,' he said.

She looked up at him, a deep blush staining her cheeks, and something inside him roared in satisfaction. She was remembering last night too.

She had been beautiful.

He could teach her.

Fire, excitement, licked along his veins. He could teach her. She would be a beautiful student. And she would...

No. *No.*

'William and I were discussing going for a walk,' she said.

'I have plans for the day,' Briggs said. 'No engagement scheduled whatsoever, because I am intent upon
taking William to see London.'

William looked up at him, and there was visible excitement in his eyes. William was not a bubbly child. He
did not show exuberance in the same way other children
did, and while Briggs did not have experience with other
children, he could see the differences between them
and his own son. But he had learned to accept the excitement that William felt. To treasure those moments.
For they were rare and precious when his son put his
joy on full display. And sometimes he pitied other fathers, for he felt the outward joy of their children was
so cheap they might never learn to value it. Briggs on
the other hand treated every smile like a piece of gold.

'I have a complete list of what we might do today,'
Briggs said.

'What time?' William asked.

'First it will be toast. And drinking chocolate. And
then our day will begin.'

'What time?'

And Briggs knew that he had to choose his answer
very carefully. He checked his timepiece. 'How about
we leave the house at ten thirty?'

'Yes,' William agreed.

'But you must wear shoes,' Beatrice said, looking
slightly triumphant.

'I will wear shoes,' William said, looking at Beatrice
as if she had grown another head. And Briggs could
only be amused by that.

'Can I join you?'

'For toast?' William asked.

'For the day?' She directed that question at Briggs.

He was about to issue a denial, when William turned to look him in the face, which was so rare that Briggs could not help but be completely taken back by it.

'She must come,' he said.

'I had thought,' Briggs said, 'that it would be just men.'

'But that would be boring,' William said. 'Because Beatrice is not boring.'

'*Beatrice*, is it?' Briggs asked, wondering what the boy should call her, but certain it should not be her first name.

'Yes,' she said. 'I asked him to call me Beatrice.'

'Because we are friends,' William said. 'She calls me William.'

He could not argue with this unassailable logic. It was quite annoying.

'Then of course Beatrice shall accompany us, but I will have hurt feelings that you think I'm boring.'

'I did not say you were boring,' William said. 'I said Beatrice was not boring.'

And he could not argue with that either. Instead, he found himself going down to breakfast with them, where toast for William, and coffee and eggs and meat awaited the three.

'I am pleased that we are going on an outing,' Beatrice said.

'I'm not an ogre,' he said. 'I would not bring William here and not take him to see the city.'

'But you would bring me and have me not see it?'

'You will see it in time. There will be balls...'

'That is not the same,' she said.

'Have you not been to London?'

'I have been to London once. I did not see the sites.

I spent my days shut up in Hugh's town house. And I was sent home early. For he had concerns regarding my well-being, and the quality of the air.' She did not elaborate. But she looked like she might want to.

'And?'

'I had a fit with my breathing. It upset him greatly, it was the first time I had one in a very long time. And he sent me home.'

'You find your breathing well now?'

Anger burned through him.

She should tell him these things. She should tell him it was dangerous for her to be in London.

'I'm fine,' she said. 'I have not had the same sort of maladies that I had all those years ago. I was fourteen when that happened, and I have been quite well since. Please do not make this about my illness. I find that far too many things are.'

'I will not worry, but you will tell me if you feel ill.'

'I will.'

'Are you sick?' William asked, and he looked terribly concerned. 'My mother was very sick.'

Beatrice's face contorted with alarm.

'No, William. I am not sick like that. I was very sick when I was a young child. That's all.' Except she had no real idea what kind of sick Serena was. But then, neither did William.

'Good,' William said decisively. 'I do not wish for you to die.'

'I am glad to hear it,' Beatrice said.

He and Beatrice made eye contact, and her cheeks flushed again.

He looked at William, who was now absorbed in his toast, though he had a feeling that at exactly ten twenty-nine his son would emerge from wherever it was he went to let them know that they were in danger of running behind.

'You slept well?' he asked, where he was being provocative.

'No,' she responded. 'I did not.'

There were a great many things he could say in response to that, but he decided that none of them would be in particular aid of the situation.

'I'm sorry to hear it.'

'I was lonely.'

'I could not have stayed,' he said, hearing his voice go gruff.

She looked at him for a long while. A litany of questions was in her blue eyes and he did not wish to answer any of them. 'Why?'

'Do not ask questions you are not prepared to hear the answer to.'

'Do not assume what I am prepared for. You, like everyone else, underestimate me.'

'I do not underestimate you, but neither do I forget the reality of your health.'

'Is it truly me you worry for? Or are you simply obeying my brother's orders?'

He frowned. 'I worry for you. And of course I respect what Kendal has asked of me...'

'I know my brother made it clear you must watch out for me. But he is not here. And I am fine.'

'I do not trust you to always make the best decision when it comes to your own needs,' he said.

'That is a shame,' she said. 'Because I do. And I should like it if even one person gave me the benefit of being treated like a woman. You have done so once,' she said, her blue eyes meeting his, crackling with heat. 'Is it not hypocritical to treat me only as a woman when it suits you, and to otherwise relegate me to the position of ward?'

'Is it not hypocritical of you to ask for something and then attempt to use it against me?'

'I have asked for one thing,' she said. 'With consistency. To be treated as if I know my own mind, and to be given the freedom that I feel I deserve. I did not act counter to those wishes last night. I did what I wanted.'

She wanted.

He knew exactly what she wanted.

He could give it to her.

'It is time to go.' Just as Briggs had known he would, William returned to them as if an internal timepiece had told him that they were nearing the moment Briggs had said they would leave.

He was grateful. Because he did not wish to continue this conversation. He felt perilously close to the edges of dreams he'd had years ago. That perhaps he was not so bent, he only had to find the woman who would decide to bend around him.

He could pay women to do so, but part of him had always desired...

The hunger he saw in Beatrice's face.

And yet he could not. They could not.

With Alice and attendants, they got into the carriage.

It was not just the look of wonder on William's face that Briggs found himself captivated by. But Beatrice's.

He had forgotten what it was like to look around the world and see anything new, but everything was new to her.

The sights, the sounds, they were significant to her. Special. And it filled him with a deep sense of pride to be the person to have shown her.

And of course, it was unavoidable, he could not help but compare it to the pleasure that she had been shown last night. In his arms, she had fallen apart, and he had prevented her from splintering. He wanted to know if she had ever felt that manner of pleasure before. If she had found it with her own hand. He enjoyed that image very much.

Beatrice, laying on her bed, her hand between her thighs…

He wanted to know so many things, and he wanted to show her so much more, and yet, he knew that it was impossible.

Why? You said so yourself, there are many things that can be done without producing a child.

It was true. However, while he enjoyed games of self-control, there were limits. And while he believed himself to be a man of extreme control, and in fact enjoyed that as an aspect to his bed sport, eventually, he would need to be inside a woman. That was just how it worked. He was not a man who could forgo being inside a woman forever. And if he were to play with her physically, it was possible she would be hurt by his need to take his fulfilment with other women. And it was just best, easiest, if these things remained separate.

Is it not too late for that?

It was not too late. Not if he determined in himself that it wasn't.

They first stopped at Westminster, and walked around the outside, with William exclaiming about the architecture, and offering titbits about timelines in the construction.

They went to St James's afterwards, and took a distant look around the grounds. He had no wish to be accosted by the Duke of Cumberland and forced to take part in the conversation he did not wish to have.

William took equal delight in all aspects of the way the city was put together. From the intricate network of roads to the different buildings, whether or not they were famous. Briggs knew that his son's knowledge of architecture and infrastructure was astonishing, but he had truly had no idea of the breadth of it.

There were things that William knew about London that Briggs himself did not, and even if he had known it at some point, he would've forgotten it. William seemed to forget nothing. Particularly not if it involved numbers and dates.

'I have learned so much,' Beatrice said, beaming, tilting her head back and letting the sun wash over her face.

She was a rare beauty, was Beatrice.

If she had made a formal debut in society when she should have, she would have been a diamond of the first water. Would have been considered a triumph for any man. The sister of a duke, with a large dowry, incomparable innocence and extreme beauty. It was a farce that she should be limited as she was. An absolute injustice.

She seemed happy, though, and that pleased him. Right now, she was happy.

She could be happy with him. They did not have to be at odds. He thought of her as she'd been last night, furious with him, and then fire in his arms. No. There was no reason for them to play in extremes.

He could simply care for her. While he could no

longer deny that he wanted her, there was a measure of satisfaction that stirred in him over the idea of simply...being with her.

Caring for her.

Showing her new sights, buying her new dresses.

'Rome is best,' William said matter-of-factly, with all the authority of a small boy who had only for the first time truly travelled away from home.

'I should like to see Rome some day,' Beatrice said, looking over at him.

'I have a feeling I will be outnumbered in votes for this venture,' Briggs said. 'However, I am a duke, so I don't know that I can truly be outnumbered.'

'I don't know,' Beatrice said. 'William is quite persuasive.'

'At times.'

Beatrice laughed. 'Isn't that true of all of us? It is said that you catch more flies with honey than vinegar, but sometimes it is so satisfying to speak with vinegar, that whatever the result might be is sincerely worth the diminished returns.'

'Is that so?'

'Yes. Anyway, being sweet eternally is terribly boring.'

'How would you know? You have never been endlessly sweet or biddable.'

She looked surprised by that. Did she not realise he always took note of her?

'Indeed not,' Beatrice said. 'Because I find the prospect so unappealing.'

'You are a wretched minx, do you know that?'

She wrinkled her nose. 'I quite like that. I shall take

on the mantle of wretched minx for all of my days. For it is much more interesting than poor, sickly Beatrice.'

'I doubt anyone has ever referred to you as poor, sickly Beatrice.'

'Untrue,' she said. 'It is heavy in the tone of every servant in my brother's house, and in the way my own mother looks at me. She is filled with sorrow on my behalf. I find it tiring. All I hear is how sweet I am, but what that means is that I do not fight with those around me all day every day. I have no choice in my life, and that I do not kick constantly against it has earned me the label of sweet.'

'Beatrice,' he said. 'You're not a thing to be pitied. There is much in life set before us that we are shown is the right thing, but...' He looked down at William, who was focusing on the details carved into a parapet. And he allowed him. 'I achieved everything that I was meant to by the time I was twenty-three. I had my wife, my heir. It did not produce happiness. I do not speak of William. William has brought me...'

He felt *happiness* was an insipid word, and not truly the correct one. Being a father was not an endless parade of smiling. He was a duke who could have staff members see to William the entirety of the time if he so chose, but it would not make a difference, as William was ever present on his mind, as were his concerns for him. And so he found it was best to spend time with his son. Perhaps much more time than most men in his position would. But seeing him, understanding him in this way, rather than in relayed messages from staff, was truly the only thing that actually made him feel like William would be fine. For when he saw him like this, out in the world and filled with joy, when he was able to hear about the things that sparked his son's imagination, then they connected. And then, somehow, he had a glimmer of hope that all would be well.

Still, happiness was not…

'William added depth to me. That was not there before. Being his father is perhaps the greatest challenge of my life. But it has made me a better man. Still, there is happiness outside of these prescribed roles. And sometimes there is little happiness to be found in them. My first marriage did not produce happiness.'

He needed her to understand this. Perhaps just now. As they were in public, as they were safe from it all becoming too intimate, even as he spoke of things he often left in the dark corners of his memory.

He was not being cruel for the sake of it.

It was clear to him Beatrice would welcome his touch. At least, as she understood it. But disquiet remained, in his soul.

For he had believed he had a connection with Serena, and he had been wrong.

For he had missed the signs that she was so deeply unhappy she no longer wanted to live. That she no longer loved him had been clear. But the rest…

He had not known.

And the feeling he had caused it, contributed to it, by telling her of his desires to be dominant with her in their bed, stuck in him.

They continued to stroll along the walk, the sun filtering over the grass, the flowers and the gold of the palace.

'What of ours, Briggs? Is it to be more of what we had last night?' She did not look at him when she asked the question.

She might not look at him, but he did look at her. Her bravery, her honesty, lit brilliantly by the sun, amazed him.

Shamed him.

'An impossibility, I'm afraid.'

'You regret it so?'

'Beatrice...'

'Only I'm just beginning to understand. Desire. Desiring another person, and what that means. Is it that you do not desire me?'

He curled his hands into fists, for if he did not he did not think he could resist touching her. 'If I did not desire you, last night would not have occurred.'

'I am your wife. Why should it be a complication for you to desire me?'

'Because of the rules we must fulfil for each other. Because of the way that I have been tasked with protecting you, and you can be angry about it all you like, but it does not change the way of things. I care for your brother a great deal, and promises were made to him.'

'It is not his life,' she said. 'It is mine.'

'And I'm your husband. So your life is mine now.'

'What a scintillating conclusion to have come to,' she said.

'You are mine, and that means I will care for you, as I said. I don't think you understand truly what that means.'

Of course she did. She didn't understand the deep... It was primal. The thing in him that demanded he care for that which was his. When he took a woman into his bed, her pleasure and her satisfaction, walking the line between pleasure and pain perfectly, was of the utmost importance to him. But even more, ensuring that Beatrice found happiness, that she was well-clothed and well fed, with her favourite foods...

Remember how you used to bring her sweets?

He stilled, locking his back teeth together.

And he refused to acknowledge that. The idea that all along he had been drawing her to him. Baiting her as if she were a small animal. Feeding her sweets.

None of what had happened between them was planned.

And when she threw herself at you in the library, and you slid your hand down to her arse, what exactly did you think you were doing?

He had known it was her.

Of course he had.

He was a man who paid great attention to detail.

A man who had been consumed with the details of her from the moment he'd met her.

And no, he had not thought of her beauty when she had been a girl. It had been her resilience, her sadness, her wildness.

But he had *known* her.

And he had known her when she'd gone into his arms.

'There is much you don't know of the world. We will find happiness together in it. But you must trust me.'

She looked up at him, her eyes filled with scepticism. And he could not stop himself. He reached out and took hold of her chin, gripping it tightly between his thumb and forefinger. 'You must trust me.'

She looked away. 'I don't think I can.'

'If you cannot trust me in this, you would not have been able to trust me with more.'

Her eyes flashed up to his. 'With...'

He released his hold on her. 'Let us walk this way, William. You wish to see St James's Park?'

'Yes,' William responded, never quicker with an answer than when everything was going his way.

That was not fair. It was not about getting his way, it was about being in this perfect space where there was no resistance being brought against him by the things that he found challenging in the world.

Briggs understood that. He remembered being a boy and finding peace only in books, and then in the hours spent seeing to the health of his orchids. He understood how engaging his own brain could be when it was occupied by things that were important to him.

And how difficult the world could feel when he did not connect with what was happening.

It was not a choice to be bad or misbehave, but a strange reordering of his brain, as if all of the pieces of his mind had been shoved into an overcrowded corner, leaving him in part overwhelmed and the other disconnected.

He had better control over these things now. But he still remembered when he was at the mercy of his emotions.

They turned and began to walk towards the park, Beatrice next to him, the wind now against her. And he did his best to ignore just how appealing she smelled to him. And it was nothing to do with the rose water she had likely placed just beneath her earlobes. And everything to do with the smell of her skin.

He had tasted her last night. She had been marvellous.

He would've thought that it would be the easiest thing in all the world to protect his best friend's younger sister in this position. For he had no interest in a wife, and he'd seen Beatrice as a child...

Did you?

He did not like this insidious voice searching inside himself for truth. He was not interested in his truth. He was interested, rather, in maintaining things as they were. And not allowing them to deteriorate.

St James's Park was filled with those intent on taking advantage of the sunshine, a veritable menu of societal elite, promenading so as to be seen by those who mattered. Briggs had never had the patience for such things. It was perhaps why he had married as quickly as he had done. For participating in the marriage mart, in these sorts of games, had not been his idea of intrigue at any point.

And now that he was back here, it was thankfully with a wife in tow, so as not to bring any marriage-minded mothers and their debutantes his way.

Beatrice herself looked delighted by the spectacle, and her delight only increased her beauty. He could feel the envious gazes of men around him.

Truly, these fashionable dresses with their boldly scooped necklines flattered Beatrice in an extreme fashion. Her tits were a glory. That he knew well, as he'd had them in his mouth.

Desire was like a raging beast in him, right here in the sunshine in the full view of so many people, with his son so near.

And that was something unfamiliar.

He separated these parts of his life. For him, sex and desire had nothing to do with what he did the rest of his days. It was disconnected. A service he bought. He had purposed that he would not expose himself again by sharing his desires with a woman who might not have the same needs.

Beatrice did.

She wanted the same things.

It was intoxicating.

It had been sufficient, keeping his intimate desires satisfied by whores. Beneficial for all involved.

But this was something he'd craved. Something he'd determined did not actually exist. The possibility of sharing his life with a woman who also wanted in the way he did.

It made him feel vulnerable.

It made him *feel*.

He didn't like it.

And yet he did not know if he could deny himself either.

William ran through the grass, though he did not join any of the groups of children that were about.

'Does he not like to be with other children?'

'He does not have much experience of them,' Briggs said. 'Though… I feel that if he wished to play with children, he would say.'

'He does not seem to long for inclusion.'

'No. I recall… I recall often feeling that way when I was in school.'

'When did you go to school?'

'When I was fourteen. I was taught at home by my governess until then.'

'Do you know why?'

He laughed. 'One does not question the Duke of Brigham, Your Grace. By which I mean my father. One does not speak to him also. I don't just mean now, because he is dead. He was ashamed of me, and he did not wish for me to be at school where I might reflect poorly on him.'

'Surely he did not…'

'He did. It was not until he died that my mother finally sent me.'

'What a terrible…horrible man,' she said.

'He was not a good man.'

'My father was the same.' She grimaced. 'Even if he was different with it. Though I do feel you must know a bit about the notorious Duke of Kendal, and all the ways in which Hugh has taken it upon himself to rehabilitate the name and title.'

'I do know,' Briggs said. 'It is one reason that I knew I must marry you. For there is nothing more important to Hugh than reputation. The doing right.'

'Right as society defines it.'

'It is the only way that matters.'

'Yes, so it would appear. But I wonder…'

'It does not benefit us to wonder, Beatrice.'

'But if it did.'

'But it does not.'

'But you said yourself…' She looked at William, overjoyed in his solitude at the moment, even when surrounded by others. 'That happiness is not always found there.'

'No. But you know, it is not a question of whether or not you are doing everything society dictates, but whether or not you appear to be. There are thriving parts of London that operate outside of this… This fear. Where people are… More themselves.'

'Really?' She looked very keen.

'Ladies do not go to them.'

'Do they really not?'

'Not if their husbands are responsible.'

Truth be told there were a number of ladies who went to the sort of clubs he frequented. Particularly widows. Either looking for a man in the market to satisfy them, or looking to buy a harlot themselves. Briggs found nothing particularly shocking in the gaming halls and brothels of London. But perhaps that was simply due to his own acceptance of his nature.

Of course, he had wondered, when he was young, if there was something terribly wrong with him.

That he felt equal desire to kiss a woman as he did to take a riding crop to her.

But it had not taken long for him to discover books and artwork that suggested he was not alone, and then brothels that confirmed he was not. His particular favourite memory was when he had been a young man of sixteen travelling on school holidays, and he had gone to a notorious brothel in Paris and been presented with a menu. There had been acts on it he had never even considered.

And he had tried most of them. He was a man with money and few hard limits, so there was little reason not to.

Brothels had provided the perfect venue for him to explore the darker facets of his desires, while providing him with rules.

Rules, he had learned, were essential for a man like him.

He knew the women enjoyed it too. It was why he had been so certain that Serena...

'The issue, Beatrice, is that these places truly are dens of immorality.'

'The kind of immorality I must be protected from because of my health?'

'And mine,' he said. 'If your brother had any idea that I took you...'

'To a brothel?'

Of course, it had been Hugh who'd accompanied him to the Parisian brothel all those years ago. He was becoming as annoyed with the hypocrisy of the world as Beatrice.

'Must you say that here?' he said, looking around. He knew William was not paying attention to them.

But others might be.

'He would kill you,' Beatrice said, sounding nearly cheerful. 'That is a fact.'

'I would like to avoid being killed by Hugh, and if I had wanted to be killed by him, I would have simply refused to marry you in the first place.'

'So there are all these rules of society, and half of the people in society simply do not observe them? Tell me, where is the logic in that?'

'I suppose this,' he said, looking around, 'is what separates us from the animals.'

'That and corsets, I imagine.'

'Definitely corsets.'

'I had hoped to find, when I grew up, when I married, that the world was perhaps not so mystifying and unfair. That things were not quite so inequitable between men and women. I had hoped, that there would be a magical moment when all knowledge, and all things, might be open to me. But it is not to be, is it? I will always be... I will always have to live my life half in fantasy. And not even a good fantasy, because I don't even know...' She looked up at him, her blue eyes suddenly filled with tears. 'I do not even know what I want. All these desires with you and me will be half formed. Except for that one moment. That one moment in the garden.'

She went away from him then, and knelt down beside William. Who began to speak to her in an animated fashion.

And he felt…

He felt perhaps like being a duke was pointless. Because with his status and power, he was unable to give Beatrice what she wanted without breaking his vows to Hugh, and William…

Well, none of it bore thinking about, really. He had never been the kind of man to rail at fate. The world did not care. It simply unfolded, one step at a time, and you had to take it. Or die.

As his wife had chosen to do.

No. Serena was not his wife. Beatrice was his wife.

Beatrice was his wife, and that bore thinking about.

Chapter Twelve

On the second day in London, Beatrice had walked William endlessly around the little cluster of townhomes around Grosvenor Square. They had gone out to tea on the third day, though it was unfashionable to bring a child to such a venue.

He had not lasted long. He had become fractious and it had still been worth it, if only because they had left with cloth bags filled with scones.

Which she and William had elected to eat on the floor in his nursery.

Then she had gone to her bedchamber, to allow herself to be dressed to attend her very first ball as an actual lady.

Where she would dance.

But she would only be able to dance with Briggs, as he was her husband.

The partners did switch during many dances.

She had wanted this...

She had wanted it for a very long time.

All of her clothing fit perfectly, her measurements having gone to London ahead of her, the power of

Briggs's fortune and status evident in each stitch of her clothing. The gown her lady's maid put her in was gold, with glittering beads stitched over a long, filmy skirt. The bodice was low-cut, with shimmering stars sewn around the neckline. Similar stars were fastened to her hair, which was arranged in beautiful, elaborate twists.

She felt beautiful. Truly beautiful. More so than she ever had in her life, with the exception of when Briggs had held her in his arms in the garden when her hair had been down in the simple braid, her body adorned in very little, and she had felt…

She had never thought about her own beauty. At first, she had always harboured anger against her body. For being weak. For failing her, and she had never much considered whether or not it was pleasing to look at. It just pleased her in its weakness, and that was what mattered. When she had found her secret strengths, the ways in which she endured pain…

She had begun to praise her body, for being stronger than all of the illnesses that had attempted to claim her.

A matter of perspective, she supposed. In the same way that being bled could have been nothing but an unendurable pain. She had allowed it to become something else. But this… This hurt, and not in a way that made her feel strong. Her throat ached as she stared at her reflection.

She was beautiful, and it did not matter. For she had a husband, and there would be no man that would look upon her and fall desperately in love. Least of all the man who had married her.

Briggs.

Her breath caught, sharp and hard, and she turned away from her reflection.

'Thank you,' she said to her lady's maid. 'I am ready.'

A beautiful, crimson-red pelisse was draped over her shoulders, and she walked out through the door of her bedchamber, at the same time Briggs walked out of his.

He was stunning. In black as ever, with breeches that moulded in a tantalising fashion to his body. She had so many more questions about that body than she had before. And such a great interest in what she might find beneath his clothes.

There was an intensity to his gaze when he looked at her, but just as quickly as she'd seen it, it vanished. Replaced by the cool detachment he preferred to treat her with.

'You are ready,' he said.

'Yes,' she said. 'A good observation, though I suppose I should be grateful that you did not ask if I was ready, which would imply that perhaps I did not appear to be so.'

'You appear more than ready to steal all of the attention at the ball.'

'How lovely for me. And what shall I do with the attention?'

'Allow yourself to bathe in the envy of others,' he said, his voice low, and rich. Rolling over her skin. 'For how often does one get to be the fixation of every man in a room, and the focal point of the fury of every woman?'

'I can say certainly that I have never.'

She felt as if he had just given her a compliment, but she also felt like she was trembling, so it was difficult to linger on the good feeling for too long.

'But isn't that just more fantasy? Imagining what it is others think?'

'Do you have something against fantasy?'

'Perhaps I am simply tired of it, because it is all I've ever had.' She wasn't hungry for more fantasy, she wanted real.

She wanted more of those moments she'd had with him before. Real and raw. Pleasure and pain. Physical. Not gauzy, sweet dreams.

But she did not know if he would ever touch her like that again.

It made her despair. She didn't want despair, not tonight.

She didn't want to dwell on what could be, or what might not be.

She wanted to live.

They made their way out of the house and down to the carriage. He, rather than his footman, opened the door for her. When they were ensconced inside, she felt as if all the air had been taken from her lungs. Being this close to him was... It was difficult. It created a tangle of desires inside her, and she felt beset by them.

'When I was a girl, all I could do was dream.'

'Tonight is not a dream,' he said. 'Tonight is very real.'

'You will dance with me?'

'I will share a dance with you.'

'No,' she said, firm. 'I have dreamt of this all of my life. I wanted to go to a ball and have a handsome man see me from across the room and know that his life would never be complete if he did not cross that space and take me into his arms. I will never have that. I have known that for a time now. I knew it even when I thought I was contriving to set myself up to marry James. I have had to let that go. But I ask you... I beg you… Please, give me this. If you can give me nothing else.'

She felt vaguely foolish, begging like this. But this was her life, *her life*. And everyone around her was making these decisions for her and she had tried to claim her freedom, and she had not been successful.

So if she had to beg to get what she wanted tonight, then she would.

'As many dances as you wish,' he said, his voice rough. And it sent a thrill through her body.

It was as if he cared.

And that made her hope.

When they arrived, they were swept into a glittering ballroom, replete with frescoes of cherubs, not half so lovely as the ones at Maynard Park. Nor as scandalous as the ones at Bybee House.

But they were nice all the same.

It was a thrill, to be in a new place, a new ballroom. To be at a party with different people.

And to actually be part of it, rather than standing on the fringes. It had not been long ago that she had been at her brother's house party and got herself ruined. And she did wonder how her reception might be.

It turned out, there was no need for worry. Briggs was ushered immediately into a group of men, and Beatrice was summarily captured by their wives.

'I did not think that he would ever marry,' said a woman who was introduced to Beatrice as Lady Smythe.

'No, assuredly not,' said Lady Hannibal. 'He had confirmed bachelor neatly stamped across him.'

'Well. Circumstances…'

'Oh, yes,' said the Viscountess Roxbury. 'We heard all about the circumstances.'

And Beatrice awaited the judgement.

'Clever girl,' the Viscountess said. 'It was the only way one could ever snag him. To catch him in such a fashion, particularly when he holds your brother in such esteem.'

And she had the feeling that she had been talked about, at length by this group of women, as she suddenly realised that the banter that went around the circle felt a bit rehearsed.

Still, she did not get the sense that they wished her ill, nor that they disliked her, only that they were fascinated by her.

'Well, I… I have known Briggs for a very long time.' She realised that she had referred to him by his rather familiar nickname, and that she ought not to have done so. Not in this group. 'The Duke of Brigham,' she said. 'His Grace. I have known him for quite some time. And he is a man I hold in great regard.'

'How can one not hold a man whose riding breeches fit him so in high regard?' said Lady Smythe with a curve to her lips.

Beatrice felt a rash of possessiveness. She did not appreciate the lady leering over her husband.

Particularly as Beatrice herself had not seen him out of his breeches.

The idea sent a slam of indignation and something else through her, and it made her feel warm all over.

Still, she found a way to keep her smile pasted on her face, and then, mercifully, the topic of conversation turned to other gossip, and Beatrice found she quite enjoyed it. She felt very much a part of this group in a way she had never much felt a part of anything.

It was a strange sort of revelation. She had not realised how much she wanted this. An evening of feeling enchanted. Of feeling... Normal.

They did not know that her and Briggs's marriage was not what it seemed.

They were treating her like a married woman. Like someone for whom the mysteries of the universe had been unveiled.

They were treating her like an equal, and not like a poor, sickly thing.

And then it was time for a waltz, and Briggs turned, his dark eyes connecting with hers as he closed the distance between them. 'If you'll excuse us,' he said to her new friends. 'I owe my wife a dance.' His eyes never left hers. 'More than one.'

A tremor went through her body, as he took her to the dance floor, and brought her into his arms. He had said he owed her a dance, but there was a promise beneath the words that felt heavy. That made her stomach go tight.

It was a lively dance, and she could not help but laugh, in part because she had forced him to partake.

And soon, he was laughing also. They spun and twirled across the floor, and she delighted in what a strong grip he had. And what a wonderful partner he was.

Oh, he was wonderful.

She studied the lines of his face, that square jaw, those dark eyes with long dark lashes.

And his mouth. She had tasted that mouth. Had shared intimacies with him only three days earlier that she had never even imagined, much less shared with anyone else.

And he'd felt hers.

But suddenly, she had the thought. That there were other women here who had tasted him. Who had perhaps experienced greater intimacies with him than she had done.

The very idea made her feel small. Ill. And terribly sad.

But she would not focus on that, not now. For that was fantasy. That was speculation. What was real was this moment. Where he held her in his arms. And the music wound itself around them.

A sweet, piercing melody that seemed made just for them.

It did not matter that there were other people here. None of that mattered. He had wanted her to focus on what it was like to be the envy of others, but she found she did not care. She did not care. She only cared what was. What was happening. And what was happening was that she was being held by Briggs. What was happening was that she was so close to him her air was made up almost entirely of that spicy masculine scent that was him, and only him.

She looked at the strong column of his throat, at his Adam's apple there. And she became unbearably conscious of wanting to lick him.

They danced together for longer than was fashionable. She was grateful for it. Because there was no other man she wanted.

And that, she realised, was the real sadness. Not that the fantasy of meeting someone else was dashed forever. Had she ever truly wanted to meet someone else? No.

The saddest thing was that she had married Briggs. And it was something that part of her... A small corner of herself that she would never have allowed voice... Had secretly dreamed could be true. Because from the first moment he had ever brought her sweets, she had found him to be special. And she had wanted him most of all.

And there was not a fantasy left, because he was her husband, and yet she could still never truly have him.

But tonight he's dancing with you. Tonight you have this. You have lived in so many painful moments. Should you not fully live in this one?

And so she did. She allowed the music, and his arms, and the steps, to become the only thing there was.

Briggs was overwhelmed by her. She was beautiful, and when she had removed her pelisse upon entry, she had revealed the extent of the gown's secrets. He had wanted to kill the men he was speaking to, friends from school, for that matter, over the way they had allowed themselves to hungrily take their fill of her gloriously rounded bosom.

He couldn't blame them. He might've done the same had they possessed a wife of such great beauty. It was just that they did not. There was not a woman in the entire room that could hold a candle to Beatrice.

And the way that her face lit up as they danced... It ignited something inside him.

And he felt nothing but fury. At himself. At the world. But more than that, a fury at his own willingness to succumb to the helplessness of the situation. For he was not that man. It was certain he did not waste time railing at the world, but that did not mean giving in either.

He wanted her. He wanted her.

More than wanting to sink into her wet, willing body, though he did want that, he wanted her pleasure.

And he wanted her submission.

She had been made for him, as far as he could tell, nearly training herself in the art of pain all of her life.

She understood it. She understood it in the way that he did.

But there was an intense and rare gift to be found in the exchange of it.

And she was correct. It was her life. It was her life, and she had every right to decide what she wished it to be.

There would be nothing to stop her from taking her pleasure with other men, except that those men would not know how to satisfy her.

He did. They were perversely, innately made for each other.

And he wished to see just how far that went.

The only thing more unfashionable than dancing with one's wife for the entire evening was to be seen sneaking out of the ballroom with her.

But when that dance ended, he realised that it was the path he had decided on.

'Let us take a walk,' he said.

'A walk?'

He had this moment to turn back. But she was here, and she wanted to be his. He felt it. He knew it. She had said it with her mouth, had shown him with the way her body desired him and if he found her strong, and wild, and brilliant, ought he not also to believe her?

He knew there was a chance it was his weakness, his selfishness winning out. Remnants of the boy he'd once been, who had wanted nothing more than to meet a woman who might understand him.

That did not exist, that love he had once believed in. He was no longer naive enough to believe one person might accept all the ways in which he was different.

But Beatrice wanted this part of him. And so he would give it.

He was powerless to do anything else.

'Into the garden.'

'Is there a garden?'

'There always is,' he said.

'Oh,' she answered. 'Why is that?'

'Without a garden, there would be no garden path for rakes to lead innocent women down, would there?'

'Hugh has warned Eleanor about such things.'

'But never you?'

She laughed, hard. 'I think Hugh would never have thought he would have to.'

'He should have. Perhaps you would've stayed clear of me.'

'I did not know it was you.'

'Did you?' he whispered.

She shivered beneath his hold. He had not meant to issue that challenge, but he had done so. 'Walk with me.'

They walked out through the large double doors and into the dark of night. The moon was only a silver sliver, and the stars were all alike, but none of them were as compelling as the ones in Beatrice's hair.

They had entranced him all evening. Beckoning him to unpin her curls and fill his hands with them. With all of her stardust and glory.

'Briggs...'

'Didn't you want to live your fantasy tonight? Of

going to a ball? Of having a man meet your eyes across the room and find you irresistible?'

'Yes,' she said, her voice a choked whisper.

'I find you irresistible.'

She looked at him, her eyes wide, glittering, even in the moonlight.

'You don't mean that.'

'I do, Beatrice, or we would not be out here.'

'I thought perhaps you just wanted to walk.'

'As much as I want to walk, I could take one in Grosvenor Square whenever I wished. I don't wish to *walk* with you.'

'What do you wish for me?' she asked, her voice hushed.

They walked deeper into the garden, and he knew that they had to be deeper there before he risked answering her question.

'What do I want from you?' he asked as soon as the hedgerows enshrouded them completely. 'Everything. Nothing less. I should have you kneel before me, Your Grace. I should have you do whatever I ask. Beg me to take you in hand and punish you for being such a temptress.'

Her breathing had quickened, he could hear it. Feel her pulse moving through the two of them. 'You are in bad need of a punishment for what you have done to us both, don't you agree?'

'I don't… I don't know.'

'You don't have to know. You must only answer, yes, Your Grace. That is the only answer that will do.'

The pause she took was only a breath. A twinkle of starlight and nothing more, but it felt like an eternity.

'Yes,' she whispered. 'Your Grace.'

Flames licked at his veins. Arousal pulsing through him so dark and heavy he thought he might be drowned by it.

They turned the corner, and he found a bench, perfectly situated there in the garden, such a private spot. And it was a bit early yet for others to be making their way out here for trysts. At least he hoped so.

And even if not.

She was his wife.

'But here we are in a garden,' he said. 'In all things I have in mind for you... Not here.'

'Why are you teasing me?' she asked, her voice breathless.

'I am very, very serious,' he said. 'I can assure you.'

He gripped her chin, tilted her face up, and kissed her. He had kissed her before, but it had been nothing compared to this. This was... He was not being careful with her. For the way that she looked at him, the way that she acted as if he had done her harm by not finishing what they had started in his garden back at the town house...

Tonight would either inflame her desire for more or would cure her of her need for him altogether. Either way, it would be fun. The kiss was bruising. And she gasped as he licked deeper and deeper into her mouth, bit her lower lip, before sucking it hard.

She did not have any skill. But what she lacked there she made up for in enthusiasm. She was gasping, arching her body against his, trying to get closer. Trying to get everything.

'Be still,' he said.

And she responded. That note of authority in his voice made her entire body go limp against his.

'I will give you what you need. I promise.'

She whimpered, and he bit her lip again. 'Do not doubt me. Trust me.'

He moved his finger down to where the fabric of her dress met the plump flesh of her bosom. He pushed his finger beneath that gap, letting it drift around that curve, and he felt goose pimples break out over her skin.

He knew that her nipples would be tight beneath her undergarments. And he wanted deeply to pull the top of her dress down, reveal them and suck them again. But, not now. He would not risk exposing her so thoroughly here.

A light touch was not his preference, but he could tell that it tormented her, and that, he did enjoy.

'Please,' she begged. 'Please.'

'You will not get more until I say. You will not get release until I allow it. You are mine. My wife.' The words sent a lightning bolt of arousal through his body. 'Your satisfaction is my responsibility. It is also your reward. And it will not be claimed before I allow it.

'You know what I mean, don't you? Your release. What you experienced when you shattered in my arms in the garden.'

'Yes,' she whispered. 'I understand.'

'Have you ever felt that before? When you are alone in your room, did you ever put your hand between your legs and stroke yourself?'

'I...'

'You're a clever girl. You discovered that pain makes you feel powerful. That it thrills you. Did you discover how much touching yourself between your legs could thrill you?'

She shook her head. 'No.'

'I see. And what is it you do? When you're alone in your room? What is it you do when you cannot sleep?'

'Sometimes... Sometimes I dig my fingernails into my palms. I do that when I am afraid. I was doing it the night of the ball, when I was trying to get up the courage to...'

'I see. So you have given yourself pain, but never the pleasure to go with it.'

'I like it,' she said.

'Good. So do I.'

'Do you... Do you give yourself pain?'

He chuckled. 'No. I like to give it.'

And he could see, in that veiled expression, there in the garden, that his answer terrified and thrilled her all at once.

'But right now,' he said. 'There is something else. Something else I must do.'

He lowered his head and scraped his teeth along her collarbone, and he hoped, belatedly, that he had not left a mark. If so, she would have to retrieve her pelisse immediately.

He enjoyed residual marks on a woman's skin from lovemaking, but he admitted that marking one's own wife before having to go back into a ballroom was likely not the best thing.

He sat her down on the bench. And it was true, he preferred a woman on her knees before him, but, he had always known the power inherent in what he wished to do to her. So many men refused. Or were not skilled in the act.

And he had found that there was as much power to be had in branding a woman with pleasure, as guiding her in doing the same to him.

There was a tipping point, where pleasure could be used as torture, and this was one of the most effective ways he had found to do it.

They would not have infinite time here. But it would be enough.

He knelt before her and began to push her dress up over her knees. She locked them together.

'What is the matter?'

'I...'

'So sweet,' he said. 'You really are an innocent, aren't you?'

She nodded. 'You know that I am. The only ways in which I am not innocent are ways I was marked by your hands.'

'I delight in that,' he said. 'I should like to mark you all over.'

'Briggs,' she said, shivering.

'Spread your legs for me.'

'I...'

'Spread them.'

She did so, and he pushed her skirts up the rest of the way, revealing that delightful triangle of pale curls at the apex of her thighs.

And his mouth watered.

'You are beautiful,' he said.

He pressed his thumb against that source of her pleasure that he knew was there, smoothed it in a circle, and listened as she cried out in pleasure.

She was wet.

Their kiss had done its job. Their conversation had done its job.

He shifted, pressing two fingers against her swollen lips down there, trapping that little bud there between them, rubbing his fingers back and forth, careful to avoid what she really wanted.

She was moving her hips back and forth, desperately seeking more.

And he loved it. Gloried and revelled in it.

Then he put one leg of hers up over his shoulder, and another, bringing his face down so it was a scant inch from the glorious, wet heart of her.

'Briggs...'

But he did not allow her to speak. Did not allow her to say the next word. He fastened his mouth to her, moving his tongue in firm, rhythmic strokes across her flesh.

He knew what she wanted. And he would give it to her. Almost.

He feasted on her, deep, long. Until she was panting, her fingernails digging into his shoulders.

He found no particular pleasure in that, other than knowing that she was desperate for him. And for what only he could provide.

He took her close to the edge, then denied her. Pushing a finger inside her narrow, tight channel as he continued to feast on her. Took her to the edge, and then pulled back, pulled away.

She was mindless with need. Begging.

'Soon,' he said, working his finger in and out of her body. 'Soon you can come.'

'Please,' she said.

'Not yet.'

'Please, Your Grace.'

Her words shot all the way to his sex, causing it to pulse.

He wanted her. Wanted nothing more than to satisfy

the ache in his loins. Instead, he pushed another finger into her body, and bit down on her. She screamed, her orgasm sending a shock wave through her body, and then his.

And when it was done, he sat down on the bench, gathered her up in his arms and held her close while she sobbed out the rest of her pleasure. Held her until she quieted.

Then he rearranged her skirts, made sure that her hair was in place.

'I cannot possibly go back in,' she whispered.

'Why not?'

'I… Not after… You…'

'Yes,' he said. 'I have no such qualms.'

'How nice for you. But that was singular for me.'

'It was singular for me,' he said, tracing his thumb down the side of her face. 'You are extraordinary.'

'I don't understand.'

'You were right. You are mine. And…'

'I never said I was yours. You have said it. Frequently.'

'All right. You were right in that this is your life. And as I have some measure of control over it… Dammit. Beatrice, I like to see you happy. I did not like the idea that once we left here tonight the joy that I saw on your face here would end. And selfishly… The way you look in this dress…'

'You like the dress?'

'I am bewitched by it.' It was nothing less than the truth. Except, perhaps it was. Because perhaps it had less to do with the dress and more to do with her.

'Thank you,' she said, restless.

'Thank you,' he said, feeling amused. 'That's your response?'

'I am flattered,' she said.

'Beatrice...'

'What now?'

'Tonight? Tonight we will go back inside, and you will enjoy this ball all the way to the finish. We will go home. You will sleep. Tomorrow morning, I will have your favourite breakfast made.'

'You would not ask what my favourite breakfast is?'

'What is it?'

'Eggs. Bacon. And I like pastries and jam.'

'All of them will be delivered to your room. Where you will take it as a queen. Then you and I will talk. And I will explain to you what will happen. What we will do. What I enjoy. And what our limits must be. And then... Tomorrow night after supper, when William is settled... I will show you.'

'Briggs...'

'Do you want this?' He could hear the intensity in his words, but this was the most important thing. That she was giving this freely. With no reservation.

For he would lay out his every desire. His very soul.

And he had to know she would accept.

'Yes,' she said.

'You don't even know what I offer you yet.'

'Because I trust you, Your Grace.'

The words sent a surge of desire through him.

'Wait until I tell you everything. And then you may agree to it. Or not.'

'I want more of this.'

'It will not all be this, little one.'

'Will it be more of what we had in the garden at the town house?'

'Yes. And more.'

'I enjoyed that.'

'Good.'

'What if I wanted…? Tonight. What if I wanted more tonight?' She leaned forward, placing her palm flat on his chest, and he nearly felt dizzy with desire. He felt nearly overcome by his need to have her, and that was… Unusual. Typically, he had much better control over himself than this. But she was doing something to him.

Something he could not afford to allow her.

'No,' he said, keeping his tone gentle.

'You wanted me to be honest with you. And I feel… Wonderful, but… Unsatisfied.'

He could relate.

'It is of no consequence what you feel. You will learn to wait. And you will learn to wait until I tell you that you may have more. You must prove that you are able. You will prove your strength by waiting.'

'I have always known I was strong,' she said. 'It is others who have assumed that I am weak.'

'Then prove it. Prove to me that you are strong enough. To wait. And take whatever I have in store for you.'

'Yes, Your Grace.'

When she woke the first thing she became conscious of was the smell of bacon.

She opened her eyes slowly and looked to see a tray beside the bed. A massive tray. Absolutely laden, not just with bacon, but with a near mountain of pastries that exceeded her every expectation, and certainly her every request.

The second thing she became conscious of was the fact that this meant he had kept his end of the bargain.

And that meant...

That meant the rest would be coming too. The rest. She still didn't know what all of it was. But he said that he would explain it to her.

A rush of giddy joy filled her as she sat up in bed and reached out for the bacon.

She felt both lighter and more carefree, and more mature than she ever had in her life. What had happened last night had been a fantasy brought to earth. The sort of garden she had found escape in as a girl.

She had now found true desire there as a woman. Had found the truth of dreams fashioned into reality.

A need created in her, and satisfied so thoroughly she would never be able to forget either.

He was giving her what she wanted. He was. This was a real life. This life with Briggs.

It was hardly like *Emma*.

Okay, perhaps not. Perhaps it was not like *Emma* at all. He was, of course, an older man who had known her for quite some time, but there was no... It was not love, this thing between them.

And she would not claim to have had great expectations of love, not in her life. Not when she had spent so much of it being so desperately aware that she was broken.

There were some similarities of course, between the novel and her life. In that Briggs was a long-time friend of her family, and several years her senior.

But... She could not help but think about all the

qualities that she had always liked about Mr Knightley. He was assured in his authority. And that was what she liked about Briggs.

His certainty. His authority. It had been what had always drawn her to him. Like a magnet. It was not simply that he was the best-looking man that she had ever seen, though he was. It was more.

A strange sort of twist happened low in her stomach.

It was an odd thing, what he'd said to her last night. That he liked to give out pain.

But then, she supposed she liked to receive it, and if there was a person in the world who seemed made to receive pain, ought there not to be someone who enjoyed giving it?

It was as if they were two halves of a whole. Though that she and Briggs were each other's half seemed…

Overly romantic.

She did not know how to reconcile the soft romance of books she had read with what seemed to exist between herself and Briggs. Last night he had done things to her that she had not been aware existed. Exactly as he had done to her in the garden here only two days earlier.

He was teaching her, without ever saying so, that there was a dimension of life she was not conversant in, and she desperately wished to be. But he had promised that she would be so. After this.

After tonight.

The thought made her nearly wild with nerves.

It was also somewhat pleasing.

She did wish that Eleanor was here. She would like very much to speak to her. To warn her about the sorts of intimacies that men like to take. Eleanor would be shocked.

For the first time in quite some time, she thought of Penny. Her friend who had been engaged at one time to Hugh.

Had her Highlander done these things to her? That strange group who had carried her off?

Penny, by all accounts, was happy. At least, she had indicated as such in her letters, when she had arranged for them to find help for a young Scottish girl called Mairi. Hugh had generously provided a reference for her to get into a very good school. Even though he was not ever going to forgive Penny for what he viewed as a transgression, he would not pass on any sort of harm to an innocent girl.

And once he had heard of Mairi's plight, of the violation she had endured that had left her with child…

She sat there, stunned for a moment.

She had been left with child by a man who had… Taken something from her.

She had only vaguely understood these things, and her brother's fury. But now she understood slightly better. She had wanted everything that Briggs had done to her, and she wanted to get more. One thing that was evident when he held her was his strength. And how greatly it overpowered her own. How easily.

If a man wished to force his attentions on a woman, there would be nothing she could do to stop it. How terrifying. How utterly horrible to have such intimacies taken when you were not desirous of the touch.

Oh, yes, she was discovering new pieces of the world.

She looked out at the pile of pastries, and the great brick of butter on the platter.

She smiled as she thought of Briggs.

He was… He was not gentle. It was what she enjoyed

about his touch. It made her feel strong. He did not treat her as if she was breakable. When she was in his arms, she felt like a warrior. Like what she had always longed to feel like. But he was purposeful. Never once did she feel as if he might push her beyond that which she could stand. He seemed a man innately in touch with her limits. She trusted him implicitly.

When she had finished eating, her maid came into the room and told her that His Grace had requested she have a bath.

There were new scented oils to put in the water, and she luxuriated in them for a long moment, until she emerged soft and smelling like a rose garden. She was perfumed down beneath the first layer of her skin, and there was something about it that thrilled her. Because Briggs was preparing her for his touch. And she wondered… Would he strip her completely bare tonight? Press his body against hers. Would he be…?

She had yet to see him naked, and she wished greatly to do so. She had thought him beautiful all these many years, and to see the promise of all that beauty fulfilled…

It was a prospect that sent a thrill of need straight down between her thighs. She did not enjoy feeling cosseted, not usually. Because she associated it with being put away. Kept cloistered in her childhood bedroom.

This was different. She was being exceedingly pampered, but it was in aid of being presented to him tonight. And so she allowed herself to revel in it in a way she never had.

She took her lunch on the terrace that overlooked the

garden, the solitude beginning to press in on her. And she wondered when he would arrive to speak with her.

She did not fully realise when she began to understand. That this too was part of it. This anticipation that he built. The way that he positioned her, so that she spent these many hours wondering when he would appear, and exactly what would happen. The way that she obeyed him, even though nothing was stopping her from going wandering through the house and searching for him.

It was practice. For tonight. For the ways that she would need to obey. Because as he had said earlier, if she could not trust him in these sorts of things, then she would never trust him enough for the two of them to engage in greater intimacies.

She read, and lounged, and found indulgence in the act. Did not feel like a prisoner. Rather, she felt like royalty. She tried to see to her usual tasks. Spent some time with William and coaxed conversation from him about the sights he had liked best so far in London.

And all the while the anticipation built, excitement twisting her stomach, and also firing up that space between her legs.

Briggs.

His name was like her heartbeat. And, oh, how she wanted him.

Finally, at four o'clock, he came into her room.

He looked positively disreputable with his shirt collar open, and his strong chest visible there, a smattering of dark hair sprinkled over his muscles.

She was transfixed. By that white shirt, the tan skin beneath, the tight, black breeches, and his leather belt.

'You've been enjoying your day?'

'Yes,' she said.

'Good. You did exactly as I asked, which is also good.'

She felt replete with joy beneath his praise.

'Have I pleased you?'

'You have not begun to please me.'

He walked over to the bed. 'Explain to me all you know of the mechanics of what a man and woman do together.'

'Only what you have said. Only what we have done.'

'I see. So you do not understand that a man puts his cock inside of a woman and spills his seed in her and gets her with child?'

'I... I did not. No.'

'Where you were wet for me.'

She shifted. For she was wet. For him.

'I see.'

'That is the limit. We will not do that.'

'Oh,' she said, feeling hurt and disappointed, even knowing that she shouldn't.

'Last night, you were satisfied, were you not?'

'Yes,' she said.

'We will continue to endeavour to find your satisfaction, it is only that we will not fully consummate the union. Out of deference to your health.'

'I find that greatly disappointing.'

'We will recover. You may have my mouth there. Fingers. Mine and your own. I will pleasure you. And you will pleasure me.'

'And how might... How will I do that?'

'I will teach you to use your mouth on me.'

'You said... You said you might punish me.'

'Yes. Most especially for this situation we find ourselves in. I find that should be appropriate. You will tell me if it becomes too much.'

'Okay,' she said.

'I am not jesting. I will take you under my hand, and I will do so firmly, but if you do not tell me when you have been pushed to your limits, there can be no trust between us. And if there is no trust between us these games do not work. You and I must have the utmost respect for your limits or we cannot push you to them at all.'

'I promise,' she said, thrilling at being able to offer him this promise. At telling him the truth. He was very proud of her for all of the times that she had been truthful with him before. And she would continue to please him in this way.

'Then we will see one another again at dinner.'

She wanted him to stay. She wanted it to happen now. To push forward and get it over with.

She wanted the mystery unlocked. She wanted all to be revealed.

But he was going to keep her suspended in the rapture of anticipation, and she could not decide if it was brilliant, or a sort of torture. Perhaps both.

'Your brother cannot know,' he said.

'Do you honestly think that I'm going to speak to my brother of such things? He cannot even speak to me of the sorts of medical procedures that I have endured. For it all involves breaking open my skin and bleeding and things of that nature. And I dare say he does not wish to know so much about his own sister's body. He would not like to know what his friend wishes to do with it.'

To her surprise, Briggs chuckled. 'Yes. I suppose that's true. But I have no wish to be called out.'

'You've married me.'

'Your brother knows what I am. He knows how I am. He tolerates me, though he finds me to be debauched beyond what he personally would ever…'

'My brother is no saint, though he might conduct himself as one in public. I'm not a fool, Briggs. He could not maintain a friendship with you and remain a spotless lamb. It is only us ladies that are expected to be so.'

'By comparison to your father, Beatrice, believe me when I tell you that Hugh is exemplary.'

He defended her brother with great ferocity.

'Yes, I know.'

'I apologise. I should not have spoken out of turn about your father.'

'It is true, though. My father was a libertine. And perhaps… If I'm very honest, Briggs, I believe that there was more than enough information to be found around my house, and if one looked too deeply into the nude nymphs in the books at Bybee House, to educate me well enough.' She saw the real truth in that now. She had brushed against it earlier, but it hit her deeply now. Along with the reality of what her mother must have felt.

I want him and despise him in equal measure…

That made her ache, for she knew what it was to want now.

What her mother had lived with, always, was the reality of what she'd felt when Briggs had abandoned her for the brothel.

But Beatrice had been too sheltered then to know.

Her mother had known.

No wonder Beatrice had done her best to shield herself then.

She breathed out, a shaking sigh. 'But when it came to anything my father was involved in, I did not want to know. I sensed somehow that whatever capacity he... He disrespected my mother greatly. He disrespected the title. It is something that Hugh has worked a great deal to undo.'

'You are correct,' Briggs said. 'He has worked very hard to fix what your father has done, but it is not why I hold him in such esteem. I went to school late, as you know.'

'Yes.' She confirmed this with some hesitation, for he had mentioned it before but she could see now that she had missed something.

Something of what he had been trying to tell her.

'I did not know the other boys. I was the son of a duke, it was true. But I had not been raised around children, and I did not... I did not find it easy.'

She could not imagine that. Briggs was one of the most charming men she had ever known. At least, when he was intending to be. He could also be hard, and frightening, it was true. She liked him that way, if she were honest. But when he was engaged in discourse in public, he was nothing if not the consummate rake. Witty and delightful, and jolly good company.

'I did not find it easy,' he repeated. 'I did not understand how to speak to children my own age. I was left largely to my own devices, and my interests were... My own. Hugh practically trained me to make friends.'

'Hugh did? It seems to me that you are the one most likely to make friends of the two of you.'

'I am a fast learner,' Briggs said. 'A good study. A brilliant mimic.'

'Modest as well.'

'No. Never that. I will always be grateful to him. I will always owe him a debt. And this... Is surely a poor way to repay him.'

'Or,' Beatrice said, 'it has nothing to do with him. I should like it if what I want could be separated from him and what he wants. Utterly and absolutely.'

He looked at her, long and hard for a moment, his dark eyes glittering, darting back and forth as though he was doing some sort of mental calculus. 'I see you as a whole person, unto yourself,' he said. 'Please don't mistake me. But your brother will not. And... As I said before... He knows a bit too much about me for... For him to avoid making assumptions about our relationship should he discover we have one.'

'Of all the things, Briggs, who would've thought that the scandal you truly wish to avoid is someone thinking you have shared intimacies with your wife.'

His lips curved up at the corner. 'It only shocks you because you know so little about me.'

'You can tell me more.'

'We will speak after dinner.'

'I should hope that we will speak at dinner,' she said.

'Yes. But that is where people will see. And who we are away from others... That is where true honesty is, is it not?'

She shivered. He spoke the truth. She knew that he did.

It was as he'd said before, about polite society. All of these people who enforced proper behaviour... They did not necessarily engage in such behaviour themselves, and what was more, they knew fully that beneath the glittering veneer of the surface, many others did not. It was meant to corral the innocent and the powerless, more than anything else.

But who they were when they were alone… That was freedom.

And as long as she got a taste of it… She could endure it being between herself and Briggs only.

In fact, it felt lovely. Like a secret. No, not a secret, like a precious gem that you might conceal, so that it is not stolen or tarnished by anyone else. Like something too beautiful to give away.

And then he left her. And she knew that now, she had only to wait until after dinner.

Where he would make good on his promises, and she would find…

She did not know what exactly. Only that there was a certainty, bright and burning in the centre of her soul, that told her tonight she would find a piece of herself.

Chapter Thirteen

Dinner was a study in torture. But Beatrice had come
to accept that torture was a part of all of this. At least,
between herself and Briggs.

That feeling that she was guarding something precious and rare intensified. Yes, she was disappointed
that he was going to withhold… Certain things from her.
Not even thinking further down the road that he would
be withholding a baby from her, but that there was an
intimacy that was… That he was not willing to give.

But she had the sense that it was a common intimacy.
Perhaps, the most common. And that what was about to
take place between herself and Briggs was not common.

They ate dinner across the table from each other, and
she did feel as if they were strangers, observing customs
that simply didn't matter. That had nothing to do with
the two of them. With Briggs and Beatrice and all that
they could be. All that they would be.

For the first time she felt… Special. Not like she
might be less, but that she might be more.

She was careful not to overfill herself, and when
dinner was finished, she stood.

'I am ready to retire,' she said.

He looked up at her. 'Is that true?'

'Yes, Your Grace,' she said, using his title making her stomach tense. It should not. Only that there was a way he seemed to enjoy hearing it. And it was different, different to the way it was spoken in common conversation, where it was just an observation of his title, an expression of what was due to him. There was something else. Something deeper.

She went to her room, and her maid helped her dress for bed. She looked at herself in the mirror, and she wondered. If she was truly enough of a woman to entice him.

It had been one thing in the beautiful ball gown, with all those stars in her hair. She had been bewitched by her own reflection, so she imagined that she had a much better chance of bewitching Briggs in that state. But now... She just looked very much like herself.

The night that he had left the brothel, he had gone to engage in these activities, but had not done so. So no doubt that had played a part in his enticement towards her. That was why the nightgown had been sufficient then. But would it be enough now?

Would she be enough?

Or would she fall short?

No. You will not fall short. He trusts that you will not.

She looked at herself, and straightened her shoulders. He did not see her as an invalid. And she would not behave as if he should. This was what she had always wanted. For someone to see her as strong. As whole. Even recognising that he must... That he must behave differently with her... He was still not keeping himself from her entirely.

And that must be a testament to his desire. And to the way that he saw her.

And then the door opened. And he was here.

He was dressed fully for dinner, rather than in that state of partial undress that he'd been in when he had come into her room earlier today. For some reason, it gave him a look of unfettered authority, and that excited her all the more.

This man who seemed to be the embodiment of all she had ever wanted. It made her bold. If he was all she wanted, perhaps she could be all he wanted as well.

'Do you know,' she said, 'all of my life, men have stood in authority over me. I suppose that is the fate of all women. Whether it be my father, my brother, or the physicians who attended me when I was ill, men have always dictated my fate. And so I cannot fathom why it is your authority that I find so beautiful.'

He paused, a muscle in his square jaw jumping. 'There are two reasons. The first is that you know I will exert my authority in ways that will bring you pleasure. I take no joy in causing pain for the sake of it. Nor do I exert my will simply because I can. I was born with a title. I was born with authority. England is filled with spineless men who have been given power because of the structure of the world. And women must subject to this authority because of how they were born. You… You willingly submit. And that is what gives me the power. That is what makes it mean something. And I will not abuse that. The second thing is related. Choice. You choose this. You choose it because it is something you want. And I granted it because I know it is something you can handle. It is not the de facto power a man has over his wife. Nor the power society gives a man over a woman. Rather this is something we choose. Something we make the rules to. Yes, in this bed, you give the power to me. But when it comes to the rules of the game, the ultimate power lies with us. Not what anyone tells us we might have. And that is intoxicating indeed.'

She shivered, absolutely and completely held captive by his words. For he was right.

This was power, the likes of which she had never known. For the fire inside him was stoked high, taken to a place that he was not in utter command of. She had command of his desire. He was here because he wanted her, and she did not doubt it. She did not need stars in her hair or a dress that flattered her bosom. She simply needed to be her.

The right fit to who and what he was. And that was innate inside her. The same as the illness that had threatened to take all the joy from her life. It made her grateful for herself. For strength, for the innate pieces of who she was. All that she could be.

Beatrice was enough for this moment. And after being wrong, not enough, not strong enough, according to all of the people that surrounded her, for so many years of her life, it was more than a revelation.

'The first thing I think you are strong enough to handle, is learning to please me.'

He closed the distance between them, his gaze fierce. 'Turn around.'

She obeyed, turning her back to him, and she flinched slightly when he wrapped his fingers around her braid. But he did not tug her hair, as he had done before. Instead, he gently released it from its fastenings and let it fall loose around her shoulders. His touch was gentle, and it made her shiver. Because it wasn't gentle as if he was afraid she would break. It was gentle like a gift. The calm before a storm that she knew would rage and push them both to a breaking point.

Then he began to loosen the ties at the back of her nightgown, and it fell, slid down her body in a slither of silk, and pooled at her feet. Leaving her completely naked. His touch was gentle as his fingers skimmed down the line of her spine, down to her backside, where he squeezed her tightly, an echo of what had occurred in the library of her brother's house, though so much more intentional. And with no barrier between them.

Tears stung her eyes.

There was nothing between them. Nothing except for his own clothes.

And she thought that perhaps she should be embarrassed, but she wasn't.

Physicians had seen her nude from the time she was a child. It had been a necessity. Part of a life spent practically bedridden.

But he was not examining her body like a thing. Rather he touched her as if she mattered. As if she meant something. Rather he touched her as if she was both fragile and strong all at once. And beautiful.

She was not ashamed. Not embarrassed.

He dipped his fingers between her legs, stroking her in the most intimate of places.

She was wet, but she found that did not shame her either. He had made commentary about that. About her wetness. And he had made it only sound like a good thing. Something that pleased him. And she did so wish to please him.

He turned her to face him, and all the breath left her

body in an exquisite rush as he examined her. His eyes filled with an intensity that she gloried in.

This was not the cold examination of a doctor. This was the desirous look of a man.

He took two steps away from her, never taking his eyes off her as he sat down in a chair positioned by the fireplace in her bedchamber. Without taking his eyes from hers his hands moved to the falls of his breeches, and he opened them. And her throat tightened, went dry, as he drew himself from his clothing. He was... Well, as suspected, the statuary in the garden had nothing to recommend it when compared to Briggs.

He was large and thick, and... He was beautiful.

How she longed to see all of his body, completely uncovered for her pleasure. But she had a feeling it was something she would have to earn. And she would do her very best. He said he was going to teach her to pleasure him, and suddenly she wanted that more than she wanted anything else. More than she had ever wanted anything before.

'Come to me,' he said.

'Yes,' she said.

'Your Grace,' he said.

She recognised that it was a correction. Firm and gentle. And it made her feel...everything.

'Yes, Your Grace.'

A smile curved his lips, and she took that short trip to stand right in front of him, feeling deliciously exposed beneath the intensity of his gaze.

'Get to your knees,' he said.

She obeyed, without thought, going down to her knees in front of him.

'Good,' he said. 'I'm going to teach you how to plea-sure me. I want you to take me in your mouth.'

She was not shocked. After all, he had done the same to her in the garden and it had been exquisite. Why should he not enjoy the same intimacies? Their bodies were not the same, but surely there must be something in the taking of pleasure that they had in common.

And she wanted to... She wanted to give him some measure of what he had given to her. She did. She wanted him to feel the glory that she had felt. And if she could do for him what he had done for her, she would feel...

If she could make him shake, if she could make him cry out. If she could make his body unravel itself at that moment of release, then she would do so. It was all she wanted in that moment. The ultimate test of her strength.

And so she leaned forward, darting her tongue out over the head of his cock. He was lovely, and he tasted wonderful, something she would not have imagined. But she loved the feel of him beneath her tongue, be-neath her hands. His skin soft and hot and hard all at once.

She had lived a life repressed. She had lived a life shut in. And this was her moment. The door was flung wide. And she was free. Running with no regard in the moonlight, her hair flying behind her as she swung as high as she wanted to on the swings. This was all of that, and it was more.

It was that thrill she had felt when she had first climbed a tree, when she had fallen. When she had sneaked away to be the person that she could only be when she was by herself. That girl who wanted to be daring. Who wanted to have everything that every other girl had.

She was that girl now. But she had Briggs. And she wasn't alone.

She took him deep into her mouth, and revelled in the groan of pleasure that escaped his lips. She had him. She had him, as he had her.

And the realisation emboldened her.

He put his hand on her back, centred at her shoulder blades, then wrapped his fingers tightly around her hair, before twisting it around his hand, and tugging.

She cried out.

'Don't stop,' he commanded. So she did not. She fought against his hold, and pinpricks of pain broke out across her scalp, delighting her, spurring her on.

And she found that his pleasure seemed to echo inside her. That his need was almost greater than her own, and the counterbalance of pain on an exquisite knife's edge that kept her present.

He began to arch his hips up to greet her, the tip of him touching the back of her throat.

She welcomed that too.

She was lost in it. In him. The tug of her hair, the thrust of his arousal, the escalating need between her thighs.

She moved to touch herself, to get some sort of relief from that building pressure there.

'No,' he said, tugging sharp and hard. 'You may not pleasure yourself. Not yet. I will take my pleasure first.'

She shivered, then went back to focusing all her energy on him. And then suddenly, the bucking of his hips became wild, and they both unravelled together.

He growled his release, and she swallowed him down, as naturally as if she had trained for it.

And then, she found herself being propelled back, as he righted his breeches. Disguising himself from her.

'You did well,' he said. 'But it is not enough to re-deem you. You must receive your punishment.'

'Must I?'

'Yes. You must, because you were strong enough to withstand it.'

'Yes, Your Grace.'

And then she found herself being picked up, turned over his lap. His large hand over the globe of her rear again. He smoothed his hand over her skin, before re-moving it. And when he brought it back down, it was with a resounding crack.

She cried out. Pain spread over her body, wildfire. And before she could catch her breath, he did it again, and again. But something about the pain brought her focus between her thighs, and the bright hot ache of pleasure there.

And she could not tell where the pain ended and the pleasure began. Where the heat turned from a violent fire to an unending need. For it was all the same. Twist-ing and curling through her body. A torture she never wanted to end. Except she couldn't endure it. She was wiggling, shifting against him, trying to escape, and trying to get closer all at once. Trying to grind the cen-tre of her desire for him against his muscular thighs.

'I need…'

'Not yet,' he said, bringing his hand down on her hard.

She trembled, shook.

And she found herself going to that place, that glorious place in her that she had built as a girl.

Where no one could touch her. No one and nothing. Because she was the queen of the palace inside her. Because she could handle anything. She could withstand.

Because she was strong.

Because she was a warrior.

She was not weak. She was not broken.

She could take this. She could take him.

It went on and on, and she began to find everything fuzzy around the edges, both more and less real. She felt wholly and completely connected to her body while also somewhere outside of it. But she was not alone. And that was the most revolutionary aspect of this. He was with her. They were in this together. It was not something being done to her, it was something they were both experiencing. Something holy and completely theirs. That brilliant diamond that she would protect from all else. From all others. It was Beatrice and Briggs, and only them.

And then, he moved his hand, pushing his fingers between her legs and thrusting them deep inside her. She cried out at the invasion, which was perfectly and wholly what she needed. She was slick and accepted him easily, and he thrust forward and withdrew in a steady rhythm, until the combination of being filled by him, and the lingering staying on her flesh tipped her over the edge into a total and complete release.

She found herself shaking violently, unable to stop, babbling incoherently. She grabbed for him, and he gathered her up in his arms. And oh, this was what had been missing. Always. Always.

There had been pain. There had been pleasure. And

now he was cradling her as if she was the most precious, singular thing.

He picked her up and carried her over to the bed, where he settled against the headboard, and cradled her naked body across his hard thighs, smoothing his hand up and down her bare back.

'You've done well,' he said.

And she went limp, burying her head in his chest as she wept. Piteously and gloriously.

Somehow it was both of those things all at once. As she became both weak and strong in his arms.

'Briggs,' she whispered.

'Sleep, Beatrice.'

'Will you stay with me?'

'Yes.'

And after that, she knew nothing more.

Chapter Fourteen

Briggs did not have a restful sleep. He stayed on top of the bedclothes, fully dressed, with Beatrice curled safely beneath the blankets, nude still.

She had been beautiful. Accepting everything he had given with more strength than he had imagined possible. It was not just that she had withstood it, but she had enjoyed it. Had wholly and completely been his in that moment.

She had surrendered to the pain, and had found that glorious place where pleasure intersected with it. And her release had been brilliant.

And he had felt...

He had given her pieces of himself he had worked for years to hide. The truth of his childhood.

The truths of his needs.

Had she rejected them...

It would have been a rejection of each and every piece of who he was.

He had never shared that part of himself so completely with a woman who knew him. He had only ever come close with Serena. And Serena had been... She had been horrified. She had rejected his touch, his...

Desires. She had found them and him far too animalistic. She had never been one to give herself over entirely to the marital act, but when he had attempted to introduce more she had...

She never would have taken him in her mouth the way that Beatrice had done. And Beatrice had done so with an enthusiasm unmatched by any whore.

Though the whores he had consorted with certainly evinced a certain measure of enthusiasm, when one paid for the pleasure, one could hardly be certain as to whether or not it was authentic.

It had never mattered to him. One thing he liked about the transaction was that there was no rejection involved. There were no grey areas.

He never felt exposed in his dealings with prostitutes because it was simple. He asked for what he wanted, and if they did not wish to provide, they were under no obligation to, but they did not get their money.

With a wife it was different.

He had been young, and he had been naive, and he had been certain that they could forge a marriage much different than his parents. One that included trust and fidelity.

And that she could see to all his needs. Instead, she had found his needs appalling. After that day she had never shared his bed again, and of course, he had never pressed himself upon her. He never would have.

An essential piece of his desire was the willing supplication of the woman he wanted. He would not, and had not, touched his wife in a manner she had found distasteful.

But Beatrice had not found his needs appalling.

Beatrice stirred, soft and sleepy, and he reached out and touched her.

And the moment his fingertips connected with her hair, so silken and lovely, he imagined gripping her hips from behind, then tugging her hair back as he thrust into her from that position.

No. That was…

It would endanger her. There was a risk, even with precautions, and he could not take those risks. He would not even allow himself to think of it.

It created in him too large of a feeling, and he did not wish it to exist in him.

They had found plenty of pleasure with each other. They had found plenty of pleasure last night.

She turned and looked at him, a slow smile spreading across her face.

'Good morning, Your Grace.'

He could not help himself. And it was not often that he could not help himself. So… He simply gave in. And he kissed her. On those soft, luscious lips. Her cheeks turned pink, and she smiled. 'It was not a dream.'

'No,' he said. His chest went tight. That she could find what had passed between them to be like a dream, rather than the waking nightmare his first wife had found it…

'I was afraid that I would wake up and I would be alone. And I would still be Beatrice.'

He frowned. 'What does that mean?'

'The same Beatrice. The Beatrice I always am. The Beatrice who is always alone, and certainly has never been touched so by a man.' She looked up at him. 'You make me feel… Incredible.'

And his stomach went tense, only because he understood.

It was why he was not Philip.

It was why he was Briggs.

So he did not have to feel the same.

Her lips curved into a smile and his thoughts stopped.

He could only stare at her, marvel at the fact that she fit with him in a way he could never have quite imagined. Had it been before him all this time?

'You astonish me,' he said. 'Innocence should not take to these acts with such fervour.'

'Do I offend you with my fervour?'

She looked upset, and he did not want her upset. He resisted giving her yet more honesty, but she had been accepting of him so far. And he would hate to cause her distress simply because he was unwilling to speak of the past.

'To the contrary. I find you exceptionally pleasing. It has just not been my experience.'

'Oh,' she said, looking away. 'Your wife.'

'I'm sorry. If it upsets you for me to speak of her...'

'I believe I said that to you last time she was mentioned. It does not upset me.'

'Are you jealous, Beatrice?' Beatrice's eyes suddenly filled with tears, and she looked away from him. He frowned. 'What is it?'

'She gave you things I cannot. She gave you a child and she...'

'*You* give me things that she would not,' he said. 'And that to me means more.'

She seemed pleased by that. And he was glad that he had found some way to ease her concerns. He did not want her to be concerned. He wished for her to feel utterly and completely safe and cared for. He wished for her to feel completely satisfied in the aftermath of all they had shared.

'We will go out today.'

'Did you have obligations?'

'Likely,' he said. 'But I am here in London with you and with William, and we should go again. To the park.'

'I would like that,' she said.

And he liked to see her smile.

They went their separate ways, dressing for the day, and he sought out William, and ensured that the boy ate his breakfast.

He also decided to give the governess the afternoon off.

'We shall be together as a family today,' he said to William.

William looked pleased in that way that he often did. A small smile to himself. And Briggs felt as if he was… As if he was actually doing better than his father. It bothered him that the feeling mattered. It bothered him that it existed inside him, this desire to best his old man. And yet it did. He had not been aware it was quite so strong until now.

They got in their carriage and made their way to Grosvenor Square. They had packed a picnic for the afternoon, and he found himself slightly bemused by the fact that Beatrice had found a way to get both he and William to willingly participate in something both had said they would not. She might belong to him, but she had done a fair amount of changing the way that he lived.

She was very small for a revolutionary, and yet, he could not help but think of her as one.

'You are a warrior, Beatrice,' he said.

She looked at him, her eyes glowing. 'I am?'

'Yes.' He nodded. 'If I had to ride into battle, I would want you by my side.'

The flush of pleasure on her face pleased him immensely. And he was so focused on it, that he looked away from William for just a moment, and when he looked back, he was gone.

'William,' he said, looking around, trying to scan the group of children that were running about the edge of the water.

He spotted him finally, holding his deck of cards, and speaking seriously to three other boys. Something inside Briggs went tight. And he sat back, poised to act.

He would not intervene. Not if he wasn't needed. It was up to William to speak to other children if he wished to. And he ought to. It was a good thing. An expected thing.

But then one of the boys took hold of William's box, and flung it to the ground. And after the box, the cards.

'You're weird,' the other boy said. 'No one cares about Rome.'

'You're addled,' said another boy, and gave William a shove, and Briggs mobilised.

'You better find your governess,' he said, moving forward, and the boy looked up, his eyes going wide, and Briggs knew enough to know that the boy must have a father in the peerage, because he clearly identified Briggs as a man of great authority, his entire face going pale.

'I... I...'

'Is your governess about? Because she should seek to teach you manners, as you clearly have none.'

A woman came fluttering across the field. 'I am very sorry,' she said.

'You will do well to tell this boy's father when you give an account for his day, that he insulted the son of the Duke of Brigham. I will not allow for such a thing.'

'Sorry, Your Grace,' she said, 'so terribly sorry.'

He bent down and picked up the box, and all the cards, dumping them back in rather carelessly. And then he thrust them into William's hands. 'Take these.'

William was silent, his countenance dimmed.

They went back to the blanket where Beatrice was standing, looking outraged.

She knelt down. 'William,' she said. 'Are you all right?'

'He will be fine,' Briggs said. 'But you must…'

But then William shattered. He burst into tears, leaning against Beatrice as he wept.

'William,' she said, bringing him down to the blanket and holding him to her chest. 'It's all right. It's all right.'

'Don't cry,' Briggs said, his breath coming in shallow, angry bursts.

If the other children were to see William weeping, it would only make things more difficult for him later. He could not be remembered as that boy. And this was the exact thing he had feared. That he would find censure among other children, and it would be impossible for him to be known as anything else. And he might not be so lucky as to find a friend like Hugh who would come alongside him, who would be patient with him when he had outbursts. Who would…

'If you do not wish for other children to pour scorn

on you, then you must learn to speak only of things that they care about. You must listen to them, not speak endlessly about things that they do not care about.'

'Briggs,' she said. 'He's a boy, and he loves those cards. The other boys, they were the ones at fault.'

Beatrice was angry at him. This she could not understand.

This part of him.

And what he knew.

Because of course she could not. No one could understand him quite so deeply.

'It doesn't matter,' Briggs said. 'It does not matter if they were at fault, and they were. They have the manners of jackals, and their fathers should beat them. But it does not change the fact that William's tears will only make the children think less of him. It does not change the fact that... The children will do what they do. And if you are different in any way, they will exploit that difference. They will make you miserable. They will make you wish you had not been born. And so you must learn to conceal it.

'We will finish our picnic,' Briggs said.

William was still weeping piteously against Beatrice. 'William,' he said sharply. 'We will finish our picnic.'

He had successfully startled his son into stopping his tears.

'You cannot let them see that they have made you hurt.'

'But it hurts,' William said.

'It does not matter. They do not deserve your tears. Remember that. Nor do they deserve to hear about your cards.'

They ate, but he took no pleasure in the taste of the

food. Instead, he was consumed by his outrage, and the memories that it began to stir up inside him.

By the time the afternoon had worn on, everyone had left some of the incident behind. And he found some space to breathe around it.

But by the time they got back to the town house, he felt restless. And when William went to the nursery, he dragged Beatrice to her bedchamber, and unleashed more of the same on her from the night before. He took his pleasure, and she took hers, and when they were through, she laid her head on his lap, and spoke softly. 'Surely you cannot mean to have William never mention the things that he loves to the other children. You made it sound as if it was something he should be ashamed of.'

'It is not that he should be ashamed,' Briggs said. 'I am not ashamed of him. I'm not. But it does not matter if I am the proudest father in all the world, children will only see difference. And they will... Attack it like savages. It is who they are. It is what they do. They cannot help it, I suspect. It is innate. To make for the vulnerable, to make them wish they had not been born.'

He could remember being shoved to the ground by an older boy in the village when he'd been a lad. The boy's mother had been horrified because of who Briggs was, not because of the violence itself.

But the other boy had not cared who he was.

Imbecile.

He'd spat the word at Briggs.

All because he had asked Briggs about the weather and Briggs had explained the ideal climate for orchids.

On and on he'd talked until the other boy's fist had hit his face.

It had connected in his head, the weather and the flowers. He understood now why it had not to the other boy. But not then. Then he had not understood at all.

'Briggs...'

'No, Beatrice, you must trust me. I know of what I speak.'

'I'm sure that you do. You were right about the carriage ride, Briggs. You were. It was very hard for him. But look at how he has bloomed here in many ways. Exploring the city delights him, he adores the town house, his tantrums have slowed, the new environment is actually quite engaging for him, and it is clear he takes deep joy in it. So yes, you could've protected him from the carriage ride, but you would have also stopped him from experiencing all of this. And what a terrible tragedy it would've been. And think... If you would continue to protect me in all the ways my brother wished you to... We would've been protecting me from something that made me very happy.'

He shifted, his stomach going sour. 'I do not know that I do you any favours.'

'No,' she said. 'You do. I feel... Connected. To my body. To you. I do not know if I can explain. I spent my childhood very much as an observer. I felt as if I was not part of my family. I was always at home. While Hugh was away at school, I was at home. While he was away in London for the Season, I was at home. I was like a ghost in that house. My parents often acted as if I weren't there. Unless I was having some sort of episode.

'Sometimes my mother went away for the Season. My father would bring mistresses into the house, under the guise of…them being governesses for me. He did not speak to me. He did not… He acted as if I wouldn't tell. My mother wept outside my room often. Sometimes for me. Sometimes for herself. And I always felt as if I was pressing at a glass box, outside of all of it, controlled by everyone around me, and yet somehow completely distant from them. Closed off.

'Sometimes I would be left at home with only a governess, while they went to London for the Season, and the doctor said that my lungs would not be able to handle the city. And I learned to go places in my mind. I learned to dream. To read to find something happier than what I had in reality. But… Briggs, you must know that is such a miserable thing.

'And with you, I feel everything. When we are not separate. We are not distant. It is a revelation. It makes me feel like myself. In a good way. Not in the way I said the other morning. That I did not wish to be Beatrice. You make me feel as if Beatrice is a good thing to be. And I am always astonished by that. And I should take this feeling over protection always. Again and again.' She sighed heavily. 'You are a man who enjoys pain, and if you enjoy giving it you know someone else must enjoy receiving it. It is a balance. It is…life. How do you not see that sometimes to reach beautiful things, you must *endure* pain?'

'Because these are games, Beatrice. Games played in the bedroom, and they are not true to life.'

Her eyes were soft and filled with pity. 'They are not just games. Not to me. There's something so much more.'

'Beatrice,' he said. 'I have learned how to… Be the man that I must be. I have learned that I cannot simply… That I cannot simply follow every whim inside myself. There are places where I can be all that I feel.'

'Brothels,' she said.

'In the past that has been true. With women I have a transaction with, there is a certain expectation. I can meet them. And they meet mine. But I do not wonder about behaving this way to all and sundry.'

'Quite apart from anything else it would be very shocking,' she said.

'Yes. You cannot control the way others will treat you. But you do not need to needlessly expose yourself.'

'I do not wish to see William crushed.'

'I do not wish to see William crushed at all,' Briggs said. 'I would see him protected. From anything and everything. The best way to do that is to teach him how to… How to look like everybody else.'

He knew the pain of standing out. That boy…he had rallied other children to come after him whenever he ventured outside Maynard Park.

Eventually he had stopped leaving.

Eventually he had decided he preferred being alone.

It was Hugh who had taught him how to behave.

'Don't talk about flowers all the time, Briggs.'

'I don't. All the time.'

'No, but too often. And facts about soil and sun and things other boys don't care about.'

'I do not know what else to speak of.'

Hugh had looked confounded for a moment. *'Do you like the look of a woman's breasts?'*

Shock and shame had poured over him in equal measure, as he was still coming to grips with the shapes his fantasies were beginning to take. But that at least was an easy answer to give. *'Yes.'*

*'That is something all those lot are interested in. If
you can't think of something else to say, extol the vir-
tues of a woman's figure.'*

Be shocking. Be charming. He had learned how to
do that. He had learned to be a rake.

And it had served him well.

'All I ever wanted was to be like all the rest. To be
a girl like every other. To have the same expectations
for my life. But it was not the path for me. If I were not
born with my illness, then perhaps I would not... Perhaps the things that you and I do together would not be
something I desired. But I cannot untangle those hard-
ships with which I was born from who I am with you.
From who I am all the time. So how can I say that I
wish it were not so? How can I say that I wish I were
not Beatrice? For if one thing in my life was changed,
then I might not be the woman I am here and now. And
while I might wish away my every hardship, while I
might wish that you would allow me to fully be a wife
to you... I cannot take away the risk, the concern, the
terrible things that I have endured, and keep these precious things that we have found.'

He leaned his head back against the headboard, his
thoughts a tangle. 'But perhaps if everything wrong in
my past was undone, we would not need these things.'

'Perhaps. But they are not wrong,' she said. 'If we
are both happy enough, they cannot be.'

'The only way to avoid my father's disdain was to
be something completely different than what I was,'
he said. 'My father despised me. And when I thought I
had finally found the person who might care for me as I
was, she also...found far more to despise than care for.'

He had not meant to carry on this path. Had not

meant to continue on with this conversation. It was fruitless, after all. There was no point visiting any of these wounds in his past. He had bested his father by the simple virtue that he accepted William for who he was.

Something gouged his stomach.

Do you?

He did. What he had said to William was about keeping him safe. It had nothing to do with the way he thought the boy ought to behave. He loved the way that William thought. He was interested in the things that his son was, it was only that the rest of the world would never be. And it was not the same as what his father had done with him.

Serena had solidified these truths.

His father had been the one to teach them.

'I was not what he hoped for,' he said.

'Why?' She looked up at him, her gaze filled with genuine curiosity. 'You said before your father was ashamed of you. You seem everything a man could want his heir to be. You are handsome, and clever, and there is not a single person who does not enjoy rousing conversation with you. Why should your father not be proud of you?'

'I'm not the same as I was,' Briggs said. 'I learned. I learned to be the heir to the title. I learned to become the Duke of Brigham. Obsessions and specific curiosities, inflexibility, none of it allows you to connect with those around you. I had to learn. The other children in the village, they hurt me, Beatrice. They sought to punish me for my differences with words and fists. The boys at school did the same until Hugh taught me.'

'And so William must learn,' she said softly.

'It is not something you should concern yourself with.'

'Briggs... Tell me. Tell me about your father. Tell me about you.'

'There is nothing but the man before you,' he said, and when he said it, he almost believed it. Almost believed that he had successfully become something other than he had been.

'I am all that I must be. And that is all anyone ever need know.'

He got out of bed, and she reached for him.

'I cannot stay with you,' he said.

'Why?'

'You already know the answer.'

Perhaps she did know. Perhaps she didn't. It was not essential.

She could not become essential. And this could not become bigger than his responsibilities.

Bigger than what he'd made himself.

He had to remember. Even if Beatrice accepted him in her bed, it did not erase the way he had failed in the past.

He had become Briggs because Philip had been wrong.

And he stood there in the hall, by himself, imagining what it would be like for William when he was the Duke, and Briggs was gone. The idea, the image, made him feel hollow inside.

So he put it away, and he carried on. He knew what example he must set. He knew what he must be. In the meantime, he would take care of William and Beatrice.

Nothing else mattered.

Chapter Fifteen

For days Beatrice had been beset by what had happened at the park. By how badly Briggs had hurt William, even if unintentionally. She knew it had been unintentional. But William had been… Different since it happened. Quieter.

She wanted him to chatter again.

She had a feeling if it had only been those boys that had said those things to him, he would not have been cowed at all, but his own father had told him not to speak of those things, and that was what had silenced him.

She understood why Briggs had done it. She understood it was not out of any desire to hurt him or alter him in any way. 'William,' she said. 'Would you like to take a walk today?'

'No,' he said.

It made her chest hurt.

'What would you like to do?'

'Nothing,' he said.

'Come, let's go to the garden,' she said.

She found herself the focus of his irritation, but she

did manage to cajole him outside to the garden, where he at the very least seemed contented by the presence of the statues. She had not spent much time outside since coming to London, other than when they had gone touring. She hadn't been out in the garden in full daylight, she realised. And for the first time she noticed that there was a large glass building out in the corner.

'What is that?' she asked William.

'Oh,' William said, looking where she was gesturing. 'I don't know.'

It occurred to her then that the boy had never been here before. So asking him that question was silly at best.

'Sorry,' she said. 'I forgot that you have not been here before either.'

'It looks rather like the one at Maynard Park,' William said. 'It is a greenhouse. It is where the flowers are kept.'

'Flowers?'

'Yes. Orchids.'

She did not realise there was a greenhouse at Maynard Park. Briggs hadn't mentioned. Then she had not had a chance to explore the grounds thoroughly.

'Let's go look,' she said.

William was uninterested. But she considered it a mark of progress that she was able to extract him from the statues, and convince him to come with her. They went down the path and peered through the glass windows.

It was filled with flowers. Beautiful flowers.

She cracked open the door and walked inside, and looked around the room.

She did not know the name for all of these blooms. They were exotic and rare, brightly coloured.

'I'm not supposed to be in here,' William said.

'Why?'

'It is a rule.'

'How do you know you're not supposed to be in here if you've never been to the town house before?'

'It is the rule about the greenhouse in Maynard Park.'

'It seems a silly rule. I am with you, so you cannot get hurt.'

She grabbed his hand, just to be certain. And they began to stroll through the rows of exotic plants.

She saw movement outside the glass door, and then it opened, and in came Briggs, looking... Well, he looked furious.

'What is the meaning of this?'

'We were looking at the flowers,' she said.

'William is not allowed in the greenhouse.'

'So he said, but he's with me and...'

'Out,' Briggs said.

'Briggs...'

'Out,' Briggs said, his tone clipped.

She looked at him, at his handsome, angry face, and her heart squeezed.

She did not understand this man. This complicated man who made her feel like she was flying every night, and then who left her to try to find a place to land all on her own. Who both satisfied and left her aching with desire all at once.

Briggs...

And now he was angry with her, because she had done something wrong, but he had not laid out expectations for this. And she didn't know how he expected her to know exactly what he wanted her to do about everything if he did not tell her.

He could not be so picky if he wasn't going to be explicit in his instructions.

'The plants are very fragile,' he said.

And she stopped. Because she realised that this wasn't about William. It was about him. And it wasn't even about protecting the plants, there was something else.

'We will go,' she said. 'But you must take us on a walk, and you must entertain us,' she said.

'Must I?'

'You owe us, for behaving the part of an ogre,' she said. 'We did nothing to deserve your wrath. You did not leave clear instructions for me, and I was not given to understand there was any part of the garden that might be off limits. Now you have been an utter brute, and you must make up for it.'

'You are not an authority over me, Beatrice,' he said.

'Of course not, Your Grace,' she said, looking at him from beneath her lashes and knowing it would inflame his desire. Her confidence had grown in that at least.

She was rewarded with a flare of heat in his dark gaze.

She had been correct. He liked that. Liked her deference, even when it was hardened with an edge of defiance.

And that was how she finally got Briggs to take her and William out again, and how she got William slightly more out of his shell than he'd been over the past few days.

She would have to talk to Briggs about that. About

the way he had been affected by what happened in the park. And about what she suspected was Briggs's part in it.

Afterward, they had dinner together, and then Briggs went, to his studies she presumed.

She had a letter from Hugh to read, and one from Eleanor as well. Both informing her that they were coming for the Season, and would be there in just a few days.

She knew that she should feel excited. To see her brother. See Eleanor. But... She felt selfishly upset that they were coming in and breaking up what was happening here.

She wondered how it would affect the way Briggs treated her. And what happened in her bedchamber at night.

She did not wish for that. She wanted to stay in her separate life, and she did not want Bybee House or her past to intrude.

She realised that was vile of her. But she could not help herself.

She waited for Briggs to come to her, but he did not. And finally, after becoming impatient, she went and looked in his study, but did not find him. And it was only intuition that led her down the stairs and out to the garden. Where she could see it. An amber light flickering back where she now knew the greenhouse was.

She had been right. She had been right, in her assessment of the fact that he had been trying to protect something when they had been in there earlier, but that it was not about the flowers.

This was him. There was a key here. A key to him. And she knew it. And so she stepped outside and followed the ambient glow of the light, and through the windows, she could see him. Inside, bent over one of the plants.

She pushed the door open. She did not knock, for fear that he would turn her away.

He might still turn her away, but she was already inside... He stiffened, then turned.

'Is this where you are? When I don't see you. I assumed you were in your study working away, but you're here, aren't you? William told me that there was a greenhouse in Maynard Park as well.'

'Not always,' he said.

'Briggs, why haven't you mentioned this?'

'I learned a long time ago that there are things people do not wish to hear about. It is not a mark against them, it is simply up to me to learn what people are interested in, and stick to those topics.'

'You like... You like flowers.'

'Horticulture and botany,' he said. 'The more complicated the better. The less suited to the English atmosphere, the better. I find it diverting.'

'For how long?'

He looked at her, his dark eyes intense. 'As long as I can remember.'

'These are your cards,' she said softly. She looked around. 'Briggs, do you not know that you're very like William?'

'He likes buildings. I like flowers. It is not the same.'

'It is the same. And that's why you reacted the way that you did when those boys were mean to him. People have been very unkind to you in the past, haven't they?'

'It is no matter.'

'But it is,' she said. 'Your father was unkind to you, wasn't he?'

He huffed out a laugh. 'Can you imagine how useless a man like my father would find this?'

'No,' she said. 'Because I did not know your father. You will have to tell me.'

'He hated this. He hated everything that I cared about. And I do not wish to speak further of it.'

'Why?'

'It will only bore you, and I reached my limit with how often I can possibly watch a person's eyes glaze over with boredom while I speak of things that matter to me. I reached the limit with how often I can disgust someone with who I am. I do not wish to do it any more.'

'I am not a child. I do not mock what I don't understand. I... I never had the chance to have friends, not when I was young. Maybe I would've been your friend.'

'No, Beatrice, if you had not lived a cloistered existence for you were forced to be different than others, you would not have been any different than the children that accosted William. For that is human nature. It is who we are.'

'I find that very grim.'

'Humanity is grim. There is no denying it.'

'I'm not a child now, though. I can certainly understand about this if you want me to.'

'I do not talk about myself. About...'

'I want to know, Briggs,' she said. 'I want to know you. It matters to me. You matter to me. And what matters to you will mean something. I can understand. Please, give me a chance to understand.'

'If I've learned one thing in this life it is that when

230 Marriage Deal with the Devilish Duke

you give too much of yourself away there will always be those standing by waiting to tear pieces from you. It is inevitable. My father...'

'I'm not your father.'

'Believe me, I did not confuse you with my father.'

'What got you interested in this?'

'Beatrice, this is not a wound that you can heal. I have learned to be different. I am content to see to my interests on my own time. It is not of any matter.'

'I want to understand you. And if you would deny us...'

'All right,' he said. 'You want to understand me?' He advanced towards her, and Beatrice shrank away. The intensity that radiated off him was confusing. For there was more happening inside him than she could fathom. There were things he was not saying. And it... It wounded her. Confronted her.

He grabbed hold of her arm and pulled her up against him. 'Do you pity me, Beatrice?'

'I don't understand,' she whispered.

'You pity my son, I think.'

'I don't,' she said. 'I don't pity William. I care for him. He is a wonderful... Unique child. He is not like everyone else, and that... I know what that's like. It doesn't matter whether it's because of buildings, or an illness, it amounts to the same thing. You end up on the outside looking in. And sometimes the loneliness is so bitter that you can do nothing to combat it. No, I don't pity him. And I don't pity you.'

'You might. If you knew the truth. About me.'

'Tell me, then?'

'My father wanted a son. He always wanted a son. When he had his son, his heir, his life was complete.

And then he had his spare. The problem is, his heir died. His perfect, precious heir. And then he was left with… Well, they are spares for a reason.'

'Briggs… I had no idea. I didn't…'

'My brother died when he was ten. I was two. I don't remember him. But I already showed signs of lacking where he succeeded. In every way I was inferior to my brother. And my father took every opportunity to make sure that was known. My brother spoke in full sentences by his first birthday. I could not speak when I was four. I was lost in my own mind. Often turning over concepts and problems that I could not express. I became obsessed with small things. Knots for a while. Shoelaces. Small things. Eventually, I became entranced by gardens. Plants. I wished to know all about them, how they grew and where. So I learned. I became fixated on the orangery in my family home. And meanwhile, my father was trying to get me interested in other things. Trying to get me so that I could go to school and not be… Mocked brutally for the fact that I couldn't converse about anything more complex than an orchid.'

'But you…'

'Yes. I do well now. I learned. A bad combination of isolation and my natural self, I believe, made it harder for me for longer than it might have. If not for your brother, I would never have found my way at school. I'm certain of that.

'But it does not matter.'

'It does matter. It hurts you still.'

'My obsessiveness served me well in places in my life. In school, when it comes to managing the dukedom. With women.'

She flushed. She did not want to hear about him with women.

'I might always be the spare in the eyes of my father, the son that meant less to him. That he loved less. But... I have found other ways to gain appreciation. He used to punish me. When I could not speak on the topics he wished me to.'

'Oh,' she said. And of course she thought of the way that he had punished her. Of course she thought of that. How could she not?

'You feel out of control when you're a child.'

'You like to feel in control.'

'Yes. And I also like rare flowers. They are complicated. And one must know just how to care for them. You must take great care to observe, take into account every aspect of the environment. It is not so different than what I do with women. Finding the perfect balance of pleasure and pain. Watching your breathing. Your eyes.'

He took another step towards her, and she took a step away, her bottom hitting one of the platforms that held all the plants. That section was empty, the surface clear.

'You are like an orchid,' he said. 'You are in my care. And if I fail you, if you begin to lose your colour, the fault is with me.'

She could see. She could see it. He took total control, total responsibility, after a childhood spent feeling as if he had none. And she had felt... Insecure. Unsafe. She had wanted nothing more than to feel safe. As if she could trust all those in authority over her. But her father often acted in his own self-interest, her mother was distracted—even though it was her father's fault—

the doctors… She simply had to trust that their training was as good as they said.

And all the while, things were simply done to her, and none of it… None of it with her permission.

While Briggs made her feel safe, taken care of. When he put his hand on her, she knew that it would be with the right kind of care.

She was his orchid. And he the master gardener.

'He said he wished I were dead,' Briggs said, his mouth now nearly pressed against hers. 'He said that he wished I were the one who had died.'

'Briggs…'

'And look at me, have I not done well? I've done better than him. It's only a shame that he's dead and he cannot see it.'

'Briggs.' She closed the distance between them and kissed him. Kissed him fiercely. And he wrapped his arms tightly around her, kissing her as if she were the source of all life. As if… 'I want to know you,' she said, moving her hands to his cravat and undoing it, pulling his shirt open. She knew that this was outside the realm of their games. That she was not permitted to take his clothes off. She was not directed to do anything of the sort, and if she was not directed to do it, she did not do it. But she was lost in this. And his kiss. In her desperate need for him.

She opened his shirt, pushed it down his shoulders, and he tore at the front of her dress, exposing her breasts and pinching her ruthlessly. She cried out, arching against him. She reached desperately for the falls on his breeches, bringing his cock out and wrapping her fingers around it. She squeezed him, an answering desperation building between her thighs. By now, she

234 Marriage Deal with the Devilish Duke

knew what she wanted. He would respond by pushing his fingers into her, but he never gave her what she wanted. What she craved.

She was not an innocent. Not any more. She knew exactly what she wanted from Briggs. She knew exactly what he could make her feel. And she needed it. She did not know how to reconcile all that they were with what they both had to have. His desire to protect her. Her desire to be free. The honour that he felt when it came to his relationship with Hugh, and her desperate need to comfort him. To be all that he could possibly desire and more.

He pushed her skirts up her thighs, his fingers going between her legs as he stroked her.

'Please,' she whimpered. 'Please.' She arched forward, and he set her up on that platform, her thighs spread wide. He pressed the head of his arousal to her slick folds, stroked her, made her mad with her need for him. He was teasing her with what she wanted. Him. Inside her. That thick, masculine part of him. 'Please,' she whispered. 'Inside me. Please.'

He didn't. He was still.

And something stirred in her. A need.

His name.

She felt the head of him against her entrance, stretching her. He pushed in, a fraction of an inch and she gasped.

'Please,' she begged him. Because she was desperate. 'Philip. I need you.'

He growled and surged forward, and she cried out, his strong hands gripping her hips in a bruising fashion, the hard length of him pulsing inside her.

Whatever remained of her maidenhead was torn away by his invasion, and she revelled in the pain.

This new pain. This new closeness. Him. Inside her. So deep she could scarcely breathe.

And when he began to move, it was not gentle. His thrusts were hard and wild, the platform she was on hitting dangerously against the glass walls, the sound mingling with their laboured breathing. With her gasps of pleasure. The surface of the table was rough, biting into the delicate skin of her thighs, and the sensation mingled with the feeling of him in her, and took her breath away. She was lost in this. In him. His every thrust electrifying that centralised source of her pleasure. He reached behind her, grabbed her hair and pulled as he thrust in hard, sending her over the edge, her release an endless wave that went on and on. Then he pulled away from her, stroking himself twice and finding his own release outside of her.

When it was through, he held her there, his breathing fractured. 'That should not have happened,' he growled.

She reached up and touched his cheek, a tender, swelling sensation overtaking her chest. 'But it was always going to happen,' she whispered. 'There was never anything else. Briggs, I was always going to need you like that.'

'It is not safe enough,' he said.

'You do not get to decide the level of risk I take with my life,' she said.

'No,' he said. 'You are mine.'

'I am not an orchid,' she said. 'You do not get to keep me in a glass case. I am not that fragile.'

'You were fine with the metaphor when it brought you pleasure,' he bit out.

'And it is a fine metaphor for pleasure,' she said. 'But not for my life. I ache for you. All night long. I want to be held by you, skin to skin. I wish to have you inside me. Are we not past these games? That I am an innocent and I must be protected from you. I am not an innocent. I cannot be a convenient release for your demons, and yet never receive any relief of mine.

'Do not treat me like a child,' she said. 'Please.'

'Do you not see? This is not treating you like a child, this is treating you as if you are mine, as if you matter. When I was a child I was not treated with such care. My father destroyed the flowers I spent years on. Everything. I was thirteen. He delighted in destroying my obsessions, but only after I had put enough work into them that the loss would be deeply felt. Nothing in that house was mine. Not really. I would hear my name. Echoing off the halls with rage every time he decided I had fallen short.'

His name.

His flowers.

His father had made every part of him into something he hated.

She put her hand on his face. 'I do not pity you because of the way your father treated you. I pity him. I pity that he did not know you. And what a great tragedy it would be if I did not know you either. Can you let someone know you? Just know you?'

'He knew more than anyone.'

'I should know more than anyone. I am your wife.'

'That is not what being a wife is, little one,' he said, touching her chin. Reflexively, she looked down. 'Serena did not wish to know every aspect of who I was. She wished only to be kept comfortable, to have her child...'

'You would deny me a child.'

'I am not the one who is denying you.'

'Can we not speak to physicians? Must we take the word of a man who has cared for me since I was a child, who made endless amounts of money from treating me? There must be someone else that we can speak to. At least try.' Her eyes met his, and suddenly her stomach went tight. 'Unless you do not wish to have a child with me.'

'Beatrice…'

'Is that it?' Her breath released on a jagged note. 'You do not wish to have a child with me.'

'I never intended to marry again. And my intent was to take you as my wife and never touch you. So perhaps you should just give me a moment to contend with the changes that have occurred since we initially took vows.'

She swallowed hard. 'Can we speak to a doctor?'

'Beatrice…'

'Will you take me to bed then? Take me to bed. Spill your seed outside of my body. But be with me.'

The look on his face was like torture. 'Please don't ever touch another woman.'

He picked her up from the table, then grabbed his coat that had been draped over another one. He wrapped it over her body, and carried her from the room. And then he took her into the house, up the stairs, and for the first time, into his bedchamber.

He laid her down in the centre of the bed and began to strip his clothes from his body. And she realised that she had never seen him fully naked. He never undressed entirely for their sessions.

She removed her own clothes, and lay back. Waiting.

Then he joined her on the bed, the length of his naked body pressed to hers. And she thought she might weep. From how wonderful it felt. From how much it was... Everything. Everything that she needed. And then, for the first time, they slept together.

Chapter Sixteen

Beatrice felt something like a tentative happiness over the next few days. Briggs had made love to her the same as he had done in the greenhouse several times now. She found it thrilling each and every time. It was a revelation. Having him inside her. And while she wished that he did not have to withdraw when he found his own pleasure, she was determined to continue working on him regarding a second opinion.

But today, Hugh and Eleanor were arriving in London, and while Hugh was seeing about business with Briggs at the House of Lords, she and Eleanor would take tea.

She was very excited. To play lady of the house and dress for her friend.

She wasn't even playing. She really was the lady of the house. And properly now. She was truly Briggs's wife now.

Truly.

She wanted to call him Philip again, but he had let that one time pass without comment and she had a feeling that would not be true again, and she did not want to shake what they shared together.

She held that little spark of happiness close to her chest as she examined herself in the mirror. The mint-green gown that her maid had selected for the tea was wonderful. It made her feel fresh and beautiful. Or perhaps that was sleeping in Briggs's arms at night.

The door opened and the housekeeper arrived. 'Your Grace, Miss Eleanor Hastings is here to see you.'

She walked out of the bedchamber and went down to the morning room, where Eleanor was already seated.

'Eleanor,' Beatrice said, and her friend stood, crossing the room quickly and embracing her.

Eleanor was as delicate and beautiful as ever. The pale blue silk she was wearing suited her eyes and complexion perfectly.

'How are you?' Beatrice asked. 'Please tell me that Hugh isn't being an ogre.'

'No more so than usual,' Eleanor said, looking away.

Beatrice looked hard at her friend. 'What's wrong?'

'Nothing,' Eleanor said. 'I'm here for the Season. I will find a husband. That is a good thing.'

'Yes,' Beatrice said. 'If it is what you want.'

'I'm not like you, Beatrice. I do not have an assured place in this world whether I marry or not.' Eleanor sighed. 'I'm sorry. That was not a kind thing to say. I know that Hugh demanded you not marry.'

Beatrice shook her head. 'I'm not angry.'

The doors to the room opened and the maid came in with a tea service on a rolling tray. She laid it out before them, lovely sandwiches and cakes, and two pots of tea, along with two ornate teacups.

Beatrice smiled. 'I like being married.' She thought

about Briggs, and the things that they did together, and her face went hot. 'I mean… I like… I'm pleased that I get to host you in my own home.'

'And what of Briggs?' Eleanor asked.

'He is… I care for him a great deal, Eleanor.'

'Of course you do,' Eleanor said. 'You always have.'

There was so much she wanted to say to Eleanor, but there was… She wasn't sure she could say it. Eleanor cared so deeply for Hugh that it might put her in a difficult position. But no, she would never speak of such things to him.

'I want to speak to a doctor again,' Beatrice said. 'About having a baby.'

Eleanor looked shocked. 'But they said you could not.'

'I know. But I…' She felt the colour mount in her face. She knew she wouldn't be able to hide it. 'I have been with him. Intimately.'

'Beatrice…'

'It could not… We could not… You don't understand, Eleanor. He is the other half of me. I…'

'You're in love with him,' Eleanor said softly.

The words struck a chord deep inside her that echoed like a bell in her head. Made her teeth ache, made her chest hurt.

Oh, no.

What a terrible thing to realise.

'I had hoped,' Beatrice said, slowly, 'that love would feel nicer.'

'Is he not nice?'

'He is… I cannot explain him. But please don't tell Hugh about us.'

'You are married,' Eleanor said. 'If he honestly

thinks that he is going to control the way that you and Briggs are with one another now that you are... Now that you are married.'

'Just please do not tell him. He wanted Briggs to act as his stand-in, but it is not... That is not how we are with one another. I am not his ward. I'm his wife. I do not know if I love him. I... He makes me feel as if my heart is being cut out of my chest sometimes. And like I might die if I can't be near him.'

'As I understand it,' Eleanor said softly, 'that is love.'

'You are in love with my brother,' Beatrice said.

Eleanor looked at her. 'It is impossible.'

'It is only impossible because you think it is, and there is nothing that can be done once my brother decides something. That is the only reason, and it is not a very good one.'

'I should hope that you will tell him that. Maybe you can tell him while you proclaim your love for his best friend. And speak to him about your quest for a child.'

'You know that I can't. Once something is in his mind you cannot change it.'

'Yes,' Eleanor said. 'I do know that.'

'What is between Briggs and myself is very private. I think it is love,' she said, suddenly feeling upset. Because she had imagined that love would be more like the novel she'd read, and not this bright, sharp thing that stole her breath and made her feel like she was dying.

There was no sweet romance when they were in his bedchamber. Or hers. Or the greenhouse. It was fraught and desperate. And it contained everything. Exultant joy, deep sadness, pleasure and pain. They were a collection of their most shameful, messy parts when they were together. On full display and with nothing to conceal their sharp, jagged parts. They were… They were not a couple anyone would wish to write a novel about. For it would be unseemly. Too dark. Too hard.

And yet, so much of her life had been dark and hard and she had never thought that anyone could possibly find a way to make the sting of it make sense. To make all that she'd been through into something real. Into something that mattered. But he had done it. He made her feel.

'Maybe I will fall in love,' Eleanor said. 'With someone I can have. Maybe there will be a nice second son of an earl.'

'You do not want a nice second son of an earl.'

'No. Not because he is the second son of an earl,' Eleanor said. 'Simply because I don't know how to love someone other than… Other than His Grace.'

'Since when do you call him that?'

'I must. We are in London. And there is propriety to observe.'

'Has he scolded you? Has he put you in your place?'

'He is correct,' Eleanor said, her cheeks going pink. 'We are in society, and we must behave as if we are. I am not his sister.' Beatrice looked hard at Eleanor, and tried to see if she… Had something happened?

Beatrice knew that Hugh would find that sort of connection to his ward appalling. There were several reasons that Eleanor could never be suitable for him. But she wondered…

Because one thing Beatrice had learned was that unsuitable or not, it did not matter. Not when you desired someone. Not when they desired you. Not when you fit together in ways you had not even known were possible.

Love was inconvenient. And if there was one thing

that she could learn from *Emma*, she supposed it was that. But it was often the person who infuriated you. The person who you least wanted to need.

'I'm glad you're here,' Beatrice said. 'I only have William and Briggs to speak to, and it's... I wanted someone to speak to. Really. I am sorry, I know that you... You are unmarried. But... Physical intimacy within marriage is wonderful,' she said.

Eleanor laughed. Actually laughed. 'I know about that,' Eleanor said.

'Eleanor!'

'I mean, I have not... I understand though.'

Beatrice thought that Eleanor probably did not understand all of the things that she and Briggs did together. But then, she doubted many people would. But they did. She would never share the details. They were far too personal. Far too intimate.

'I don't think he loves me,' Beatrice said. 'Or it's impossible to tell. He is...'

'What sort of father is he?' Eleanor asked.

'Lovely,' Beatrice said, a silly smile crossing her lips.

'Lovely?'

'He is. I don't know how else to say it.'

'It is hard for me to imagine him as a father. Given all I know about his reputation,' Eleanor said.

Beatrice thought about that for a moment. 'I've thought about Briggs's reputation. His reputation is both severely under- and over-exaggerated.'

It was true. Briggs was not a rake in the way that she had once imagined him to be. With her limited understanding of what that meant. He was a man of great intensity, and the desire that burned between them was anything but simple. It was the sort of thing that many people would find objectionable. Depraved even.

But it was theirs. It was theirs and it was not for anyone else to understand. Not for anyone else to approve of.

It was different, even, than the way that high society flaunted and enforced the rules they created at their own whims. For this was not about taking joy in debauchery, or in rebellion. It was about being what the other needed. It was about his honour of her strength. About her showing how safe he made her feel.

'I'm happy you're happy,' Eleanor said.

'I am not happy that you aren't,' Beatrice said.

'I will find a way,' Eleanor responded. 'You know, a woman such as myself... I have been very lucky to have been taken in by your family. It is... It is dishonourable of me to be so sad because I cannot have the impossible. I can no more take the stars down and hold them in my hands than I can aspire to be with your brother. My heart is foolish. I can go on loving him just fine married to another man.'

'You would be content with that?'

'I would be resigned to it,' she said.

'What of your husband?'

'I dare say very few men expect love from their marriages.'

Beatrice thought of that. 'I did not expect love from mine. But he is the very dearest thing in the world to me. He is so strong, so... Hard and remote. And yet I find I want to hold him in my arms and protect him from everything that has happened.'

'Does he grieve his wife?'

'No,' she said. 'He's...' She realised it as soon as she said, 'He is angry at his wife. Deeply and bitterly angry.'

'Oh,' Eleanor said.

'I know him better than I have ever known another person. I have let him do things that... And yet there is still so much I don't know.'

'I guess that is the fortunate thing about marriage being a lifetime.'

'Yes,' she said. 'I suppose that's true.'

'I can only hope I find that a remotely fortunate prospect when I'm faced with my own.'

'Let us hope a gallant and handsome man catches your eye tonight,' Beatrice said.

'Yes,' Eleanor said. 'Let us hope so.'

Briggs had not simply failed at what he had promised, he had jumped head first into an affair with his own wife.

He could not stay away from her.

Philip. Please.

It echoed in his head. When she had begged him. By name. To be taken.

He had not been able to resist. She was all tight heat and need, and every night when he sank into her he felt himself slipping further and further away from what he had promised he could be, and embracing the darkness of what he wanted.

He did not spill his seed inside her.

She was adamant that she would speak to a physician about the risk of her carrying a child.

Still, he knew that the precautions they took were no great assurance that there would be no baby.

He was primitively satisfied in the image that came into his head of Beatrice swollen with his child.

Serena had not wanted him to touch her when she'd been pregnant, and it was entirely possible that Beatrice might feel the same way. But she would not hide her body from him. That much he was certain of. He was deeply certain he would find the sight erotic.

Not thoughts he should be having in the carriage with his wife beside him on his way to a ball where her brother would be present.

She was leaning against him, her head on his shoulder. Those things were so easy for her. Casual touches.

She touched him all the time. She freely gave sweet affection to his son, and she gave it to him in equal measure. He had not realised how hungry he was for such a thing. Something as simple as touch. Not the sort of pleasurable touch they shared in the bedroom, but this simple close touch. That was simply pressure against his body, assurance that she was there.

In cutting these sorts of relationships from his life, he had lost that.

You've never had it.

'You look beautiful tonight,' he said, distracting himself by returning to her physical beauty.

The crimson gown she was wearing tonight felt wicked. It did not reveal any more of her body than anything else she wore, but there was something about the colour that felt an announcement of sin.

And he was so well acquainted with the kinds of sin that he could commit with Beatrice.

It was all he could think of. That and dragging her out to the garden for re-enactment of previous interludes in the outdoors.

'When did you begin sneaking out of your house?'

It was something that he had puzzled over recently.

For when he had met her she had seemed a pale and drawn creature, and he did not know when those things had changed. Or if she was simply very good at putting up a smokescreen.

'When I was fourteen. I would climb out my bedroom window in the night. And sometimes I thought… Sometimes I thought it would be acceptable if it killed me. Because I was so very tired of those four walls.'

'I do not find it acceptable,' he said, looking at her. For he understood now, if reluctantly, what she thought about the baby really.

She was not concerned for her own safety. She was hungry. Hungry for experience. And perhaps he could find a way to be enough.

To be enough so that she did not feel the need to have a child.

'I understand,' she said. 'But you know, every day we take risk when rising from our beds.'

'For some it is a deeper risk,' he said.

'Perhaps,' she returned. 'But life is all the dearer to me for that reason. I fought for the chance to run in the moonlight. I had to engage in subterfuge to spend time swinging in my own garden. I had to beg for my husband's possession. I had to fight for a husband at all. Do you not see how much more dear these things are to me for that reason?'

'Beatrice,' he said, his voice rough. 'You are strong. I am in great admiration of it. But…'

'You wish to protect me.'

'Yes.'

'For Hugh's sake or for mine?'

The words caught in his throat for a moment. 'For mine.'

Her breath caught, she looked away from him, and said nothing else. When they arrived at Lady Smythe's, they were announced upon entry to the ballroom, and he immediately spotted Hugh.

Beatrice was swept away by the gaggle of ladies that had taken a shine to her, and she took Eleanor along with her.

'And how are you finding London?' Briggs asked.

Hugh's expression was opaque. 'Eleanor's dance card is full. I suppose that is a victory.'

He rather sounded like he was being sent to the gallows, not like he was pleased with his ward's performance.

Something troubled him, and Briggs wished he could help. And also felt as if he did not deserve any additional insight into what Hugh was feeling, not when he had betrayed his trust as he'd done.

But you honoured Beatrice's desires.

He found that as much as he loved his friend, that mattered more.

'Full marks to you,' Briggs said.

Hugh cast an eye over him. 'And how are *you* finding London?'

'I am here. As ever. And Beatrice is getting her experience of the Season.'

'Good,' Hugh said, looking around.

'William is enjoying himself.' Normally he went out of his way to never speak of William. Not even to Hugh.

His friend lifted a brow, indicating his surprise.

'I'm glad to hear it.'

'Beatrice is a wonderful stepmother to him,' he said.

'He has… He has changed a great deal with her. I wonder what would've become of me if I'd had a mother who had cared for me so.'

He did not know why he was saying this to his friend, except that he knew what Briggs had been like when he had first gone to school. The lack of confidence he'd felt. The inability to speak to other children.

'I'm glad to hear it. That it has been something beneficial for you.'

'I would hope for all of us.'

'That is more than I expected to hear, I confess.'

'She is a strong woman, your sister,' Briggs said. It was difficult for him to keep the admiration from his voice, and then, why should he? Hugh should understand. He should understand what manner of woman Beatrice was. Woman. Because he got the feeling his friend still thought of her as a girl. And she was not. She was strong, and glorious. When the two of them made love they…

Hugh's head turned sharply, his focus suddenly diverted. Briggs followed his gaze. His ward had gone to the dance floor and was now in the arms of another man.

'I do not approve of that,' Hugh said.

'Abernathy? Why?'

'You know full well.'

'He frequents the sort of brothels that we do?' Briggs asked.

'He has a reputation for being quite perverse.'

'So do I, as you well know.'

The look that Hugh gave him went hard. 'Yes, and I have full confidence that you are not visiting such acts upon my sister or I would look at you much the same.'

Briggs ground his back teeth together. '*She* is not your sister,' he said, indicating Eleanor.

'No,' he said. 'Indeed she is not.'

Beatrice separated herself from her lady-friends, and fixed him with a bright smile. Then she looked at her brother. 'It is so good to see you.' He knew that were they not in the ballroom she would've flung herself at Hugh and given him a hug.

'And you. London suits you.'

'Yes,' Beatrice said defiantly. 'It does. I remember a time when you did not think that would be true.'

'I'm happy to be proven wrong,' Hugh said.

'Well, a strange thing indeed coming from you. I did not realise the Duke of Kendal ever thought he could be wrong.'

Her words were strong and clear. She was not saying this to him to goad him, rather she was not allowing him total control of the situation. He recognised a person playing at mastery when he saw it.

It was damnably impressive.

'In this instance,' he said, 'I am pleased to be.'

'My dear husband,' Beatrice said. 'Perhaps you should spare me a dance. We can keep an eye on Eleanor. Which I do think my brother would like. So that he can stop staring daggers in that direction.'

'I'm not staring daggers.'

'You are. Do not make this miserable for her,' Beatrice said, not allowing him to get away with it.

'Excuse me?'

'Do not make it miserable for her,' Beatrice repeated. 'Whether it be because of protection or because you do not want another man to have that which you will not take yourself, you must not make her miserable. Please let her be happy.'

'She will not be happy with him,' Kendal said, bristling, and Briggs felt utterly outclassed by his wife. Who had clearly identified something happening that he had not.

'You must let her determine that,' Beatrice said. 'You must let her decide what will make her happy.' Beatrice let out a harsh breath. 'You cannot protect people from everything. You cannot force everyone to live the life that you think is best.'

'Of course I can,' Kendal said. 'I'm a duke.'

'You are a stubborn ass is what you are,' Beatrice said. 'Come. Let us dance.'

Briggs shrugged, and allowed Beatrice to take him to the dance floor, where he took her into his arms. 'Bold of you,' Briggs said.

'Eleanor is miserable with love for him. He cannot act a jealous lover when he has no intention of ever...'

'Beatrice,' Briggs said gently. 'Even if he did see her that way, which he has never indicated to me that he does, you know he never would. She is beneath his station in every way, and under his protection.'

'I know,' Beatrice said. 'And so does she. But it does not change the way that she feels. If he truly wishes to do a kind thing for her, he must let her be happy. He must let her be.'

'Human hearts are terribly inconvenient things,' Briggs said.

'Yes,' Beatrice agreed readily. 'They are.'

Her eyes took on a strange light, and he shifted uncomfortably.

Eleanor, for her part, looked like she was enjoying

herself well enough, as she traded partners with frequency. She was extraordinarily beautiful, and even though her icy blonde beauty did not appeal to Briggs when he had Beatrice's lovely chestnut curls beneath his hands, he could see that she was just the sort of woman that many men would like. She did not have a title, or a dowry, but she was under the Duke of Kendal's protection, and he was offering quite the dowry. She should be able to find herself a good match.

Such a strange thing, to be at one of these events with a wife again. He had not fully appreciated it the first time.

He did not have to avoid women coyly trying to get his attention. Then indeed, even if there were women attempting to get his attention, he did not think he would notice.

He was brought back to the moment by Beatrice's hand on his cheek.

'You are missing from me.'

'I'm not,' he said. 'Never.'

Her cheeks flushed. 'I remember when I so looked forward to experiencing a ball. And now I find myself impatient to leave so that you and I can be alone.'

'If your brother were not here, I might take you into the garden again.'

'That I would enjoy. But perhaps I would be the one to pleasure you.'

His desire had him in a chokehold. And he knew that he should not tease her like this, not so openly. But everyone around them was dancing, and they were far too interested in their own entanglements to worry at all about Briggs and his wife.

He moved his hand up between her shoulder blades,

then up still to the back of her neck, his hold turning possessive. And he felt her shiver beneath his touch.

'A promise,' he said. 'For later.'

'I will hold you to that promise. I must warn you, I'm feeling particularly unruly tonight.'

'You shall require a firm hand.'

Her grin lit up the ballroom. And he felt it square at the centre of his chest.

'I do hope so.'

When he looked up it was because he felt, rather than saw, someone looking at him. And he was correct. The Duke of Kendal had fixed him with a thousand-yard stare that felt rather like a knife at the centre of his back.

He had been wrong then, about the interest of others. Hugh needed to find himself a woman to distract him, for Briggs had no interest in being the focus of his attention.

But then, Hugh would not find the sort of woman he liked here. While he did not share Briggs's specific affinities, what he knew was that his friend tended towards a level of roughness not ever visited upon gently bred ladies.

'Come on,' he said.

He led her out towards the back of the ballroom, to the terrace. And he sensed that Kendal was following them.

He was not in the mood to have a discussion with his friend about the details of his intimate life.

'What is it?'

'Oh, I imagine we will discover exactly what it is in just a few moments.'

'Why exactly was I watching as the two of you flirted outrageously on a dance floor?'

'We are married,' Beatrice pointed out. 'I cannot be ruined by my own husband.'

'Do not be incorrigible,' Hugh said. 'You and I both know the circumstances of your marriage.'

'Nobody knows the circumstances of our marriage but us,' Beatrice said.

And he did want to tell her to not play quite so grandly with his fate. He did like to be alive.

'Briggs, I asked one thing of you.'

'Yes. You asked me to take care of your sister. You asked me to treat her as a ward.'

'I have the sense things have changed.'

Briggs knew that he was about to cross a line. And he thought to himself for a long moment about whether or not he wished to turn back. He did not.

'Perhaps, it is simply that you are taking your feelings about what you would like to do with your ward and placing them on my shoulders.'

Hugh took a step forward. 'You bastard. You would question my honour.'

'I know what it looks like when a man burns with jealousy, Kendal. I'm not blind.'

'And I know what it looks like when a man is gazing at a woman in a way that suggests he has taken her to bed.'

'Are you accusing me of being bedded by my *husband*?' Beatrice asked. 'As if you have a say in that. As if it is yours to know? Because that is too far, Hugh. Even for you, it is too far. You may not control my life. You do not get a say in what I can endure.'

'Having a child could kill you.'

'Yes. But being married to Briggs and not having him would have killed me as well. Oh, I might've still drawn breath, but my broken heart would have hurt every time it beat.'

Hugh took a step back, a muscle jumping in his jaw. But he was only shocked enough to be set back for a moment. 'He is not a knight of the round table, Beatrice. He is a dragon. And you will end up burned.'

'Perhaps I like dragons. And fire in equal measure. You think me weak,' she said. 'And if you insist on inserting yourself into my life, then you will discover things that you may not wish to know. Not the least of which because you do not wish to know such things about your sister, but because you do not wish to find out you are wrong, and I think perhaps that is the thing that will burn the most. Do you think I fear the things that he wants? I run towards them. There are many things you don't know about me.'

'And you know exactly why his first wife died?'

Briggs took a step forward. 'That is too far.'

'If you laid a hand on my sister in the way you handle your whores then you have gone too far.'

'You would rather I stay married to a man who must seek out pleasure at a brothel, rather than giving myself to him? Even if it is what I want?'

'You cannot…'

'I cannot understand? I was bled. My skin was cut open, my… The process of saving my life was nothing but pain. Pain and isolation. What I wish to do with that life should be up to me. The cost that it took to get me here… You do not get to say how I will live. It is not your decision to make. And you will not speak so to my husband.'

'If you put my sister's life at risk, I can no longer call you a friend.'

'If you care so little for her happiness then perhaps I can no longer call you one either.'

And that was not even considering the fact that he had brought Serena into it. Her death. And his every feeling of guilt on the subject. 'Come, Beatrice. I think it is time we went home.'

'Yes,' she said.

But not before she put her hand on his face and kissed him boldly on the mouth. 'I should like to go home.'

She walked past Kendal without giving him a glance, and back into the ballroom.

Kendal stopped him with a hand on his chest. 'This is a betrayal.'

'It does not surprise me,' Briggs said, his chest feeling cut open. 'But in the end of all things, you find me as repellent as all others I have once called friends and family. But she does not.'

'For now.'

'For now,' Briggs said.

'And if she has a child, and she dies…'

The words stabbed straight through his chest. A knife to his heart. It was a deep fear, one that left him gasping for breath.

But he had seen her. What she wanted. What she was capable of.

What she craved.

He knew she would never be happy with half a life. She wanted it all.

He would be damned if he was the one that kept her in chains.

'I will never forgive myself. But you have the luxury of turning her into an object. Of turning her into a child that you must guide and care for. I have a child. I have a son, and I know the difference between being a father and being a husband. I am not her brother. I am not her father. She is my wife. And I am her life sentence.'

'Better than being her gallows.'

'She is not a child. I cannot look at her day in and day out and feel pleased with sentencing her to have a life where she is treated like she is weak and like she does not know her own desires.'

'That is a very noble way of saying you cannot control your cock.'

'Perhaps I cannot. Perhaps I want her. But you will find that she is not upset about that either. All she wanted was a Season, Kendal. For a man to look at her across the room and want her. I want her. She and I have been shaped and forged in a particular sort of fire, and I suppose the end result is that we suit each other better than we could've imagined. I am not ashamed of it. I refuse to be.'

'I wash my hands of you.'

'Then you wash your hands of her as well. For she is my wife. She is my family now. I protect mine.'

He walked away then, leaving behind the only real friend he had ever had.

And when he exited the ballroom, he saw her standing there, her arms wrapped tightly around herself. And he realised… He had her now. Whatever else.

In this moment. He had her.

They got into the carriage together, and she put her hand on his thigh. More of that casual sort of touch that lit him from within. 'I'm sorry,' Beatrice said. 'That was a terrible thing for him to say. It was a terrible thing for him to do. You are an honourable man, Briggs…'

'I'm not,' Briggs said. 'He is right. If I had honour, I

wouldn't have touched you. But I did not have honour, what I had was a desire to see you happier than you were. And I wanted you. It was that simple.'

'I am not sorry about it.'

'I know,' he said.

'He should not have brought up your wife.'

No. But perhaps now was the time when he should speak to Beatrice about it.

But he did not. He did not. Instead when they got home they did not speak. He pulled her into his arms, and made a particularly punishing night of it.

The next day, she set out to find a physician to speak to.

And Briggs decided to have a picnic indoors with William.

'Where are your cards, William?' he asked, when they were midway through their meal and he realised that his son had not produced them.

'I do not play with them any more.'

'Why not?'

'I know all the answers on them. They're in my head. Where no one can see.'

Briggs felt a twist of regret inside him.

And there were so many things he wanted to say, but he did not know how to say them.

He thought of what his own father would've done, but he couldn't even get that far, because his father would not have been here sitting on the floor with him.

He did not know how to do this. He did not know how to... How to be the right thing for people. And he was trying. Trying for Beatrice, because she deserved it. But the cost was losing Hugh's friendship. He did not know how to protect his son, and make it feel like

there was nothing wrong with him. He did not know
what things to share of himself and what things to hold
back. He did not understand how to make Briggs be a
good father.

May I call you Philip?

No.

What sort of father would Philip have been? What
if he turned around and started talking about orchids?

It was exhausting. This.

And he did not know the way around it.

Beatrice returned home; she was pale and large-eyed.

'How was your visit with the physician?' he asked.

'He said that there is always risk in having a child.
And he cannot guarantee any woman that she will survive.'

Briggs laughed. But there was no humour in it.
'Quite a measured response.'

'He does not see why I should be any more vulnerable than any other woman. We talked extensively
about my issues. The malady in my lungs, and how it
has not been as bad in recent years. He said he does
sometimes see this. The children who survive a childhood such as mine, with lungs that close off, sometimes
fare much better as adults. He said it is difficult to get
a firm grasp on how many, because very often they do
not survive childhood.'

'I see.'

'He thinks that we can have a baby.'

He very suddenly, very fiercely did not wish to share
her.

'Perhaps some day.'

'That is all right,' she said. 'I do not need one now.

But I would like for there to be no restraint between us. At least tonight.'

Desire was a beast inside him. He knew what she was asking. And tonight... Tonight he felt willing, more than willing, to take the risk. 'Philip,' she said. 'I wish for you to take me to bed.'

It was still not yet dark, but he did not care. He picked her up, right there in the entry, and carried her up the stairs, in full view of all the servants, who undoubtedly knew exactly what he intended for his Duchess. He did not care. He simply did not care. For he was out of restraint. There was none left within him. And he wished to revel in that.

He had lost one of the most important people in his life for this. For her.

And he would make the decision again. Perhaps Kendal was right. And he simply had no control over his cock. But it felt like more. It felt deeper. 'Strip for me, little one.'

And she did, with no hesitation. Removing her layers with a coy look in her eye.

She gloried in his gaze. And it made him feel like a god. She was a lady. Gently bred, cosseted too. And she would be brazen for him.

'On your knees,' he said.

She approached him, dropping to her knees in front of him, her eyes intent on his. This was nothing like the studied submission of a whore. But a gift. A gift to him that he was not certain he deserved. No. He was certain he did not.

Because she did not know about Serena. Not the whole truth of it.

He freed himself from his breeches, gripped the back

of her head and guided her to him, roughly thrusting inside her mouth.

As ever, she gave in to him. With absolute freedom. Seeming to revel in all that he was.

He stopped her before he could come. Before he ended things.

Then he picked her up and moved her to the bed, depositing her on her knees and pressing his hand firmly between her shoulder blades, so that her breasts were against the mattress. And her ass was up in the air. She was lovely like this. And he did not think he would ever get enough.

'Is this what you want?'

'Yes,' she said.

'You want me,' he said. 'You want me, and all that I am?' He brought his palm down hard on the plump global flesh, leaving a bright red mark behind.

She squirmed against him, the yelp that she made more one of pleasure than pain. 'Yes,' she said.

'For the rest of your life. You want me?'

'Yes,' she said in time with another strike of his hand.

'He was right. I am depraved. And you know that makes you depraved right along with me.'

'Yes,' she said. He timed it with another firm smack. Over and over until her every breath was in affirmation. Until she was marked by him.

Until she was shaking. And so was he.

'Philip,' she said. 'Please, Philip.'

And it was balm for his soul that she used his name. Because right in this moment he did not feel confused. Whether he was Philip or Briggs.

He was hers.

He pressed himself up against the wet entrance of

her body and thrust hard. Claiming her over and over again, the only sound in the room flesh striking against flesh. And when her pleasure exploded around him, he could not keep himself back any longer. He released hold of his control. And he let himself spill inside her.

'Philip,' she whispered. 'Philip, I love you.'

Chapter Seventeen

Beatrice was rocked. Utterly shaken.

In the space of just a few hours she had found out that she could have a baby, had seduced her husband, and had told him that she loved him.

She was laying there in the aftermath of their desire, shattered and terrified. For she had not meant to say aloud that she loved him. Not yet.

But she could not keep it in. Not any more.

She was not… She was not sorry. She was not sad. It felt right. This. No matter what happened.

'I love you.'

'Love,' he said. 'I do not… I do not even understand what that means.'

'You do not understand what love means?'

'I do not understand what it has to do with this.'

'It has everything to do with this. You are my husband. My lover. My friend. I love you.'

'You love me,' he said, his tone sardonic. 'I do not think you do. Moreover, I do not wish to have this conversation. It is… It is foolish.'

'What is foolish about it?'

'No one has ever loved me. No one. No one has ever said those words to me.'

'Briggs,' she said. Her heart squeezed. 'Philip.'

'Do not call me that.'

'You have no issue with me calling you that when you're inside me.' She moved away from him, swinging her legs over the side of the bed frame and standing.

'It's different.' He sat up, getting out of bed and standing with the expanse of mattress between them.

'Philip, just because your father could not understand you...'

'You are not the least bit curious what your brother meant when he spoke of my wife?'

'I do not wish to pry. You have not shared about your wife and...'

'Serena did not die of some ailment. Serena took a bath and cut her wrists open with broken glass.'

Beatrice took a step backwards, her heart slamming against her breastbone. 'Philip...'

'Do you know why? Do you know why she needed to get away from me? I discussed it with her. She never loved me, Beatrice. But I thought that we could still be friends. I thought that we could... I was so young, and I believed, I truly believed in my heart that my wife would be fashioned for me in some way. That she would understand me. We were not friends. She despised me. She could not see a way to escape me.'

'Briggs, I know you. I know you, and I know you never did anything to harm your wife. I know you would never have forced yourself on her.'

'It doesn't matter. Knowing what kind of monster I was disgusted her so much that she could not look at me. She could scarcely share the same space as me.'

'I do not believe it. I do not believe that she left this world simply because of what you wished to do in bed.'

'It is not that. It is merely a facet. It is the whole of who I am that is wrong. My father was ashamed of me. So ashamed that he wouldn't send me to school. My own wife could not bear me. And now you want to tell me that you love me? You, who married me because you were caught with me when you did not intend to be.'

'Yes,' she said. 'Because perhaps I was meant to be your wife all along. You were right, Philip. There was a woman who would love you exactly as you are. For your orchids and your punishments. For the way you make her feel.' She looked down at her body, at the bruises left on her skin, fingerprints that lingered from his touch. And they marked her. As his. As strong.

'You were the only one who saw the warrior that I wanted to be. You are the only one who treats me like I am not broken. So do not now reject my love. Do not now tell me that I am not strong enough for you.'

'You do not understand.'

'I do understand. But you do not like to be Philip because you still think that he is a little boy who could not be loved. And so you became Briggs because you thought that he might be someone that people would accept. The Duke of Brigham. But I love every piece of you. I love you and your being a cordial rake, and I love you when you are in your greenhouse. And I love the way that you are with your son. With our son. I love him. Because he is a piece of you. Delightful and different and nothing at all to be ashamed of. In the exact same way that you are.'

'It is different…'

'It is not different. Would you ever look at William

and tell him that he did not deserve to be loved? Would you ever tell him that he was so wrong...?'

'No. And you know I would not.'

'I know. So why do you do the same to yourself?'

'Because I...'

'Philip. Do you hate yourself so much, that you would punish yourself unto the end?'

He bowed his head for a moment, and then he turned away from her. 'Beatrice, I have wronged you. For I cannot be the man that you wish me to be. I cannot be what you desire. I can give you pleasure. But no more.'

'Can I give you my love?'

He shuddered. 'I cannot.'

'You cannot accept it. I... I am wounded by that. I will not tell you any lies. But I have spent my life locked away.' Even as she said it, she felt a deep pain stabbed her chest. 'I have spent my life being protected from all manner of pain. And you know that I now have come to seek it out. Oh, Briggs, I have felt so endlessly lost. So endlessly isolated. And I would rather stand here and live this moment than go back to Bybee House. I would rather love you and all this pain. I would rather love William. I would rather risk. And I will keep loving you.'

'Until you don't.'

His voice was flat. And he walked away. And Beatrice collapsed at the foot of the bed, weeping piteously. She felt... Utterly sad for him. For them. For all that they could be.

For all that he could have.

And even within the depths of her despair. She realised.

She was at war now. For his heart. For his very soul.

You always thought that you were strong enough to do this. You must not crumple now.

Briggs was drunk. And he was at a brothel.

He hated himself. Despised himself. And yet, he was doing everything he could think to do to push her away.

And you will devastate her if you touch another woman.

He knew that.

It was why he was simply in the dining area drinking. He had not gone up to one of the bedrooms yet, but he would. He would. He would do what he must in order to...

To what? Devastate her? So that you can prove your own point?

But it was the work. That was what he could not take. That was what he could not endure.

He did not know what magical combination of pieces of himself he had found to make Beatrice love him. He did not understand it. And he had no idea how to continue on with it.

And it would be like everyone. Everyone. Eventually, he would not be able to be the thing that she wanted, and then she would hate him. She would hate him.

As much as he hated himself.

He felt the same chilly presence that he had felt that night at the ball and looked up. Of course it was Kendal. He should've known better than to be seen at a brothel when his brother-in-law was in town.

'And what the hell are you doing here?'

'Leaving your sister alone. Is that not what you want?'

'Like hell. You bastard. I do not want you betraying my sister. That is certain.'

'A betrayal, is it? How so? If she is merely to be my ward.'

'And have you taken her innocence?'

He said nothing. Instead, he simply drank more whisky.

'You have. Wonderful.'

'What I have or haven't done is hardly your business. You must leave me to sort out the affairs of my marriage. After all, you will wash your hands of me.'

'It is only out of concern for Beatrice.'

'Do you want to know a cruel joke? Your sister thinks that she is in love with me.'

Hugh stopped. 'Does she?'

'Yes. She gave quite an impassioned speech to that effect earlier.'

'And now you're here. Drunk. Why is that?'

'Because you are right. There was no way she could possibly love me. How? How could she love me? I am debauched in every way. I am wrong. And I always have been. You helped me become the thing that people could tolerate. You helped turn me into a man who could at least walk into a room and have a conversation. One that was not about orchids. You took me to the brothel in Paris, and I found women there who enjoyed my particular vices. And with the exception of my late wife, with whom I made a terrible error in judgement, I have kept it there.

'Until Beatrice. And she thinks... She thinks that she loves me for it. For all that I am. For the orchids and everything else. How is that possible? And when will it end? Because it will end. It will have to end.'

A strange light entered his friend's eyes. 'I have little desire to think about the ways in which you connect with my sister. However, if she says that she loves you…'

'What? Now you believe it might be so?'

'You do not have a sister, so you are forgiven for not understanding why it was not something I wish to think about. The two of you together. I know too much about you. The hazard of being friends for as long as we have. We are now men who might deal in a bit more discretion. Whereas when we were boys, trying to figure out life's great mysteries, we were a bit more free.'

He could understand that. 'That is true. I'd…'

'It is not that I didn't think my sister could love you. It is that… You were right. I'm used to thinking of her as a child. I'm used to protecting her. Our father did nothing for us. She was merely a means for him to bring young women into the house under the guise of being her governess. He paid exorbitant fees to keep her alive. To physicians. That is all true. But he loved no one beyond himself.'

'And you have carried all of it.'

'I have carried all of it,' Kendal agreed. 'What I said about Serena was not fair.'

'It was something I had not told her.'

'Go home. You don't wish to be here.'

'I don't know where else to go.'

'You will not betray my sister.'

'No. Do you know… When we went to the brothel it was revolutionary for me. Because it was easy. I risked nothing to explore what I desired. It was a transaction. I have always found those things much easier than real life. But they do not last.'

'These things are not real. You cannot take them with you into your life. The women here... They don't know you.'

'Don't you see? I consider that a good thing.'

'Briggs, I never liked you for what you pretended to be. I of all people know exactly where you come from. Exactly who you are. Do you not know that?'

'It feels to me...'

'And if I did anything to harm the relationship between you and my sister, I am sorry. I handled it badly.'

'Does this have something to do with Eleanor?'

'I am everything my father was not. And that is my deepest source of pride in this life.'

'But that is not an answer.'

'It is the only answer I can give. Beatrice married you. She has taken you every way that you come. And she has said that she loved you first. If you cannot even be half as brave as my sister... Then perhaps you are not the man I thought you were.'

And after that, Hugh disappeared up the stairs, likely on his way to exorcise his own demons. And he left Briggs to do the same.

Philip.

He could only hear that name now on his wife's lips.

Philip. He had scorned himself back then. But now that he heard the name spoken by her and not his father... It felt different.

He felt different.

He left and took his carriage back home. He could not see Beatrice like this.

And as he made his way up the stairs, he heard screaming. Crying.

William.

He went into the room and saw his son laying on the floor, his cards spread out all around him. He did not need to know the details of what happened to recognise that he was in a rage. A deep despair. And that Briggs was responsible for it.

And it broke him.

He sat down on the floor, his own misery beginning to overtake him. He was starting to lose hold of all that held him to the earth.

'William,' he said. 'What's wrong? William.'

He was met with nothing but tears.

'I am sorry.' On his hands and knees he began to pick the cards up and put them back in the box. Carefully. With all the reverence he showed his flowers.

All the reverence his father had never shown any of his things.

'I should not have made you feel badly about these. I was scared for you. Because those children were unkind. But they simply don't understand. And you will find someone. Someone who will. A friend.' He thought of Hugh. 'A wife. And in the meantime, you have me. And you have Beatrice. We understand you. And we… We are very proud of you. And all of the things that you know. All of the things that you are. I was afraid because… I was afraid because I'm like you. I know a great many things about my flowers that I grow in the greenhouse. And I am interested in all of the details. But so many people are not. And I decided to make myself different so that I would not be scorned. But it did not make me happy. My orchids make me happy. What makes me different makes me happy.'

His son had quieted now. And was looking at him. He did not know if the boy understood.

Then suddenly William's arms were around his neck. Holding him tight. 'I love you.'

And he felt as if he had been taken out at the knees. Two people loved him. And had told him so. In the space of just a few hours. And he could scarcely breathe.

And it seemed so clear now. What he must do. He had to be a warrior. Just like Beatrice.

'I love you too.'

Chapter Eighteen

Beatrice was determined. To demand nothing of Philip. To not push. Because she thought deeply about what he'd said. About the ways he had felt like he must change. And she did not wish to do that to him.

She wanted to accept him. Just as he was. She wanted to be a gift to him. Not a burden.

She was sitting in the morning room when he came in.

'Beatrice,' he said. He was wearing the clothes he had been wearing the night before, the neckline of his shirt open. His beard was overgrown. He looked tired.

'Will you come with me?'

'Of course I will.'

He held his hand out, and she took it. He led her outside into the garden, but she had the sense he was not leading her down the garden path.

Not the way that he had done the night of the ball. No. He was leading her to his greenhouse.

'I want to show you.'

And he did. Every plant. Every name. Latin and English. All the ways that they were taken care of. Trivia about how they were discovered. All of it was in his brain.

'Which is your favourite?'

'I do not have a favourite. They are all of equal fascination to me.'

'You were brilliant.'

'There is nothing useful about orchids.'

'But you love them. That is why they are fascinating. It is the way that you see them that's extraordinary.'

'Beatrice…'

'Philip, thank you for showing me this.'

'I did not know how else to say… Except to say… I love you. I love you, and I am very sorry that I could not say it when you needed me to. Of the two of us, you are the stronger.'

Her chest burned. With joy. The satisfaction. With love.

'It is my joy to be a warrior for you.'

'I do not deserve you.'

'If there's one thing that I learned from being ill, it is that life is a gift. It is not about what you deserve or don't deserve. Bad things happen. The glorious things too. And what if we had not stumbled into each other's arms by the fire? That was a gift.'

'We both fought very hard to become something we were not in the end.'

'Did we?'

'Yes. You to become James's wife. Me to become Briggs. I think I will let the rest of the world continue to call me that. But as for you… I will be Philip. Only for you.'

'And I am Beatrice. And it makes me happy.'

'You are mine,' he said. 'And I care for what is mine.'

'I know you do.'

'I have some sweets for you.'

'Why do I feel as if I'm being tempted?'

'Because. You are. Now my darling wife... I feel that you should adequately show your love for me.'

'Of course, Your Grace.' She looked up at him, and their eyes met. 'Philip.'

Epilogue

There never was a man more frightened of his wife giving birth than the Duke of Brigham. Though perhaps her brother nearly matched him for anxiety. And when his daughter came into the world, with a healthy set of lungs, screaming, he could only give thanks that his wife's lungs seemed just as healthy.

The pregnancy had gone well. And the doctor said the labour was one of the easier he had ever seen.

It was true each time his Duchess gave birth. One thing he marvelled at was how different his children were, one from the other. And yet, he did not love any of them less.

William, for his part, proved to be a good big brother, though he did sometimes resent his siblings getting into his things, most particularly his cards.

The last of their children came when William was seventeen.

'I shall not like to be responsible for caring for this child when it cries,' William said.

He had just graduated first from Oxford. A brilliant mind. He had never been the most popular at school, but the friends he did have were true indeed.

'Do not worry, William. You will benefit from the practice,' Beatrice said, patting him on the head. 'After all, you will be a father one day.'

'I shall need to travel more first,' William said. 'I have a plan to visit every country and territory.'

Beatrice smiled, if a bit sadly. 'I have no doubt you will. But I will very much look forward to your return.'

'You do not have to worry, Mother,' William said. 'I will always come back home.'

And such a home it was. Full. And never conventional. With orchids and cards filled with the places they dreamed of visiting. With toys all over the floor. And a riding crop in their bedchamber. His life might not be the life that his father thought the Duke of Brigham should have. And for that Briggs gave thanks every day.

Because he did not want to be the Duke of Brigham the way his father wished him to be. He only wished to be Philip. The man that Beatrice loved.

That was his greatest joy in all the world.

Beatrice had set out that day to be the architect of her own ruin. And instead, she had saved them both.

* * * * *

If you enjoyed this book, why not check out this other great read by Millie Adams

Claimed for the Highlander's Revenge

And look out for more stories from Millie Adams, coming soon!

Historical Note

There are a great many elements in *Marriage Deal with the Devilish Duke* that were not understood widely in the era the book is set, and that is intentional on my part. Had Beatrice's childhood asthma been understood, and more easily treated, she would not have been weakened by the attempts to 'cure' her. If Briggs and his son's mild Autism Spectrum Disorder had been diagnosed, if their differences had been given a place in society, rather than the forced assimilation that was required, they would have had very different lives—especially Briggs, who I believe, with Beatrice's help, set about to make a better space in the world for William to be himself.

It is the same with Serena's mental health and James's sexuality, and Briggs's sexuality as well. As a society we ostracized and feared what we did not understand. In our modern times, there are labels for all and everything, but it is not labels (however helpful!) that truly advance society. It is empathy and human connection. Without labels, Beatrice was able to accept people as they were because of her position slightly outside society. She was willing to take someone just as they were, applying the kindest lens to them, which created space even in an era before labels. That is my deepest hope for the future. That we might meet on common ground, rather than focusing on differences. That we might greet people with love, and an open heart, for that is where real progress lies.